RHODES

THE MOVIE-MAKER

RHODES
THE MOVIE-MAKER

M. M. Gornell

Champlain Avenue Books, Inc.
Las Vegas, Nevada, USA

Published by Champlain Avenue Books, Inc.,
Las Vegas, Nevada

International Standard Book Number ISBN-978-1-943063-36-9

Library of Congress LCN: 2017909803

Cover by LAWRENCE

FIRST EDITION
2017

Printed in the United States of America

To:

Lawrence Gornell Sr.

PREFACE

Sometimes surprising and breathtaking happenings occur in the desert.

For example—heavy spring rains bring back to life a dry windblown-riverbed producing a mass of water powerful enough to snatch and carry away everything in its path.

Less dramatic, but no less spectacular—lighter spring rains turn broad expanses of Mojave Desert flatlands into multicolored and picture-perfect wildflower carpets.

And even the human hand—admittedly, via time-controlled irrigation boom operations, performs magical dust-to-beauty happenings. Indeed, with the flip of a well-switch, swatches of desert are brought alive with what seems like a flood of purple-to-blue flowering alfalfa.

But most amazingly—if you look widely, without preconception, in the right place, and at the appropriate point in time, you will find people who were swept up in the *flood* of human events, and did the most unexpected and exceptional things.

One such *flood* of human events plays out in *The Movie-Maker*. This tale is *not* a murder mystery, though there are in fact several murders—but there is little-to-no mystery surrounding who the perpetrators are. *Neither* is this tale meant to be a literary treatise addressing age-old philosophical questions or current day conundrums. This tale's primary goal is fun and escapism. *Nor* is *The Movie-Maker* a police procedural, though happenings do occur that require police activities. *Nor* is this tale an action drama even though dramatic actions do unfold. A romance? *Not exactly*, though several love stories—past and present—flavor happenings and decisions.

Rhodes—The Movie-Maker is simply one of many *human event* stories playing themselves out in the Mojave Desert along historic Route 66.

And to start this tale—*From LC's journal 1940 or so (exact date is smudged)*:

Jules says he had a dream last night, he was looking down on the new chimney he's a building from somewhere in the sky. Like an owl perched in a tree or something, and turning his head all around like owls do. Jules hasn't stopped building stuff since his early discharge from the army. And he claims his chimney is a sign of something. Don't know about that. Sometimes I think he can't stop cause of him being in Europe during the fighting. Hurt his brain. But since this chimney is so special to him, thinking I need to give him a special kind of house building present. A few stones maybe? For the fireplace front maybe? Viola will help me I know.

As for the perching in a tree thing though, would be a lie to say I sometimes don't wish myself I could fly like a bird over Shiné. See how all the hills and roads and flatlands mix with each other. And what a kick to see my castle from above. Flying ain't a thing us people can do though. And sure ain't getting me in one of those aero-plane things. Specially never will I get in one of them new helocopting contraptions. But still, it would be a kick.

In Chicago, a Couple Days Before it Started

Mugs Nightshade. He loved his name—given to himself, by himself on his twenty-first birthday. He never went through the legal bit, too much trouble. But his grandmother had nightshade growing the entire length of her chain link fence along the back alley. So when "of age," Mugs Nightshade he quickly became.

Long time ago. Me a kid on Paulina Street. For Mugs, those days persisted as a vivid purple and green nightshade-embossed memory—much cherished and carried close to his heart. He had loved his grandmother deeply—and would never forget her colorful out-of-control nightshade.

In stark contrast to those memories, this morning Mugs was looking out and down on a city he had a hard time recognizing as his birthplace. *Okay,* seeing his hometown from the observation deck on the ninety-fourth floor of The John Hancock Building was a view not available to him as a child; nonetheless, *so much has changed* since those days, regardless of the view. Contemplating the ever-changing nature of Chicago, Mugs reflexively rubbed his mouth and chin with the slender long-fingers of his left hand. Besides his name, he also liked being a "lefty," never attempting to become ambidextrous. Average height, average build, neither ugly or handsome features—his left handedness and slender fingers were his most distinguishing features. *And my hair,* he reflected bemusedly. *Still* thick like Uncle Harry's—but *still* jet-black with help from his barber Leo.

And so much hasn't changed. No question about it, past secrets had to remain past secrets: and to that end, in a couple hours he would be at O'Hare airport, standing in what he knew from experience would feel like an endless line waiting for the inevitable scrutiny. They always patted him down. He was sure his name was on some kind of "list." *Never found one damn thing though, now have they?* He wasn't fool enough to "carry" into the airport. Everything he needed would be waiting for him in Vegas. And given the current interest in his friends, even the FBI might be sticking their noses into Doc Francis's activities. *I do need to be extra careful.*

Admittedly though, doing a fixing job for Lucky Francis's kid would be a new experience, and exciting. Just like with his dad back in "the day." *Yeah,* some jobs were for money, but this was for old times' sake. And Doc Francis, Lucky's kid, was right; what was in the "old days" needed to stay in the old days. The first "Fixer" had failed. Odd that, because he knew Alex was competent. Once or twice Mugs had wondered where Alex had gone underground. His best guess was the legendary Fixer was off spending his money in the Caribbean somewhere.

For a moment, vertigo caused Mugs to hold his breath for fortification against wobbly-feeling legs. Some visitors were in glass box things tilting out from the deck. *Crazy. Not for me.* He grabbed hold of the quite firm and stationary railing in front of him, then blew out slowly. Feeling better, he took a quick look around the observation deck to make sure no one was watching and had seen his momentary uneasiness. *Can't ever be too careful,* he'd said many a time to himself, and to many a comrade. All he saw were gawking tourists, looking out and appearing quite awe-struck by what was their unique skyscraper-view of The Windy City.

He took in another deep long breath to steel himself further; *I'm going to look out there one more time.* His vertigo dutifully acknowledged, and hopefully under control, Mugs returned his attention to the towering skyscrapers that now represented Chicago. *Yep,* one more look before heading off to no-man's land.

But ironically and quite quickly, he stopped actually looking at the larger-than-life towers stretching before him in current time. Once again, Mugs found himself envisioning and connecting with his grandmother—and his sweet memories back on the Paulina Street of his youth.

Chapter One

A Day for Premonitions, Stomach Harbingers, and Magical Thinking

From LC's journal: Viola says she probably would have ended up a spinster-woman if it weren't for me. Says I'm special. Darned woman, do I ever love her for them words, always said at just the right time. I think she knows about saying all that romancing stuff from all those books she reads, and then the moving pictures from down below in Hollywood. She just loves all that film stuff too. By my mind, Viola would make a good moving pictures star herself I think. Ain't none of them stars prettier than her. I even wrote a song about Viola. Wonder what I did with it? Always been smitten with the woman.

Saturday Morning

With the body-rattling helicopter sound finally fading into the distance, Leiv shook himself. Then again a second time.

Given the brightness of the morning sun as it rose on the eastern horizon, all he could actually see from his west-facing window was the shadow of the helicopter moving across the Shiné Ridge. They were low hills, rather bland, and rolling-

1

topped rather than jagged—*barely hills at all*; but this morning they provided an uncannily perfect backdrop for the helicopter's iconic shadow as it moved slowly and eerily in the dawn's reflected glow. *Magical, almost*, he thought—then was chagrined at such a fanciful thought.

Leiv continued to enjoy welcoming each new day from his grandfather LC's especially designed and built octagon copula atop Rhodes Castle, and over the last couple of years had seen an array of what he considered spectacular sunrises. From golden shades of yellow, through dreamsycle-oranges, even reds. But this morning, the dark-grey, almost black helicopter shadow brought a dimension to Leiv's new-day-greeting he'd never experienced. Indeed, a tiny little piece of his psyche even felt like he was in a movie-like dream. *No, this is real.* He shook himself a third time and admonished himself a second time for being so fanciful. He was a former judge for goodness' sakes.

Nonetheless, he did attempt to share aloud, "Very strange," with his grandfather across what would be several generations of time and space.

"Did you see that stone chimney?" Pete Lily was becoming more comfortable speaking into his headset microphone, no longer shouting like when they first started out on his helicopter photo-shoot test flight. "Down there to the West. Just standing there by itself." He wanted to include the pilot's name in his observation—which he thought was Jack—though wasn't sure. Pete certainly didn't want to make a bad start by calling him by the wrong name.

"Yep," he heard the pilot answer. Pete waited for more words, but after a long moment passed, he figured that was all he was going to receive by way of reply. *Conversation probably not included in the price.* Besides, Pete knew images were *his thing*, and their importance was not necessarily shared by the pilot, who probably had no idea how iconic that chimney was in the morning light. Sitting where it was, highlighted by a rather unimpressive scrub-desert backdrop.

Were there even words capable of capturing the uniqueness of that lone chimney—a remnant of somebody's story? And now, with one chimney-story ended, maybe another about to start—the fireplace and chimney stood quite alone, but still majestic. At least in the desert scheme of things he was seeing below. Especially silhouetted as it was against the morning horizon. He felt a familiar tug at his heart; even a tear of appreciation almost wanting to come. *Can I bring that emotion to this film?* Pete wondered, doubted he could, but certainly planned to try. He always tried, but was not always satisfied with his results.

Even though this was a preliminary flyover, Pete had asked for the "door-removed option," just like it would be during shooting. He was aware others in the business thought him the top scene-framer on the West Coast, and he wanted to do his best. Pete also knew he *wasn't* the best photographer out there, especially when it came to aerial photography. In *this,* he was an amateur. *I am darned good when it comes to a still-cut. But this, looking down, looking out,* seeing it all from an omniscient-like view. *This is something else for sure.*

Consequently, this morning's aerial tour was quite special for him. Film school covered a lot, but not what he was now experiencing, and in his mind, there was no substitute for real life experience. And on the practical front, he certainly wanted to get everything he could out of Charlie White's generous one-thousand-dollar a day pre-production expenditure budget.

On top of his personal growth and economic concerns, Pete was once again overtaken by an all-encompassing and tenacious "awe" he'd first experienced a year earlier. He still remembered having to consciously force his eyes from bulging and his jaw from dropping as he took in the technical and artistic skill involved in a friend's aerial production.

His artistic eye retained to this day the magnitude and raw beauty of the images unfolding via his beloved film medium. He hadn't known then how looking "from above" would change and enhance his photography. *Close to an epiphany moment*, Pete thought several times since. All because a fellow photographer had casually invited him to an in-home showing of an aerial short he'd made—and unimaginatively titled "LA from Above."

But it wasn't just an artistic or intellectual impact Pete felt that night. Sometime during the viewing, he realized his whole body had slid, and was continuing to slide down into his seat—metaphorically melted by what he was experiencing. It was a visceral and surprisingly physical memory Pete had not forgotten. *Never will*, he figured. Those panoramic images were not only seared across his mind's eye, but were now also part of his physical being. How that could be, he wasn't sure; but knew it was real.

"I want to create that same kind of experience for others," he said softly into his helmet microphone-piece, not realizing he had.

His pilot's voice surprised him in his stereo earphones. "Did you say something?"

"No," Pete answered quickly and shook his head as if the pilot were looking at him, while knowing he wasn't.

Since Pete's thin lanky frame was safely strapped into the left front seat of the helicopter, in his quest for the perfect shoot, he next tried various movement routines even though he already knew he wouldn't be doing much of that—no handheld camera for this special shoot. *No*, he would be managing the controls for his gyro-stabilized Cineflex high definition camera—gimbal mounted, no less, on the helicopter's front—via a digital control panel right in his lap. Pete could feel his excitement building. Maybe even a slight adrenalin rush.

Nonetheless, it was still rather fun pretending he was making the shots with his usually omnipresent Canon—tilting his head and torso back and forth, looking up, down, and at different angles. *I was made for this.* And deciding on early-in-the-morning timing for this test flight turned out to be perfect. They'd only seen one car, a nondescript white sedan on the road from I-40 heading north. He should be able to capture the grandeur of the miles and miles of desert while avoiding "civilization" clashes with the modern real world.

In a louder tone than earlier and on purpose, Pete asked, "Done many aerial shoots?" Though this was a practical consideration out of the mix of ideas bouncing around in his brain, Pete did know he and his pilot would have to work as one if he wanted artistic success. "I'm guessing this is a good helicopter for what I want to do." All helicopters pretty much looked the same to him, though he'd seen the word "Raven" on this one. With that, his helicopter knowledge stopped.

"I know *who* you are," the pilot said. A man so far of few words, hearing the pilot actually speaking in such a forthright manner was a bit of a surprise. Especially since they were sitting next to each other in a small cockpit and talking headphone-to-headphone. "I was told you were good." Pete's pilot paused for half a moment before adding, "And demanding."

"Me?" Pete wasn't sure how to respond. *Why would, and how could he know about me?* But more importantly for Pete—if this was a view others had of him, he'd have to think about that, analyze. *Maybe make some changes.* He certainly wanted to be respected, but *feared*? For the moment though he forced himself to refocus, ignore the personality-adjustment implications of his pilot's remarks. His mind should just be on the shoot. "Just curious about the helicopter…trying to learn as much as I can," Pete tried to clarify and return to his original concern. "And I've heard a lot of stories about this desert. Thinking about what I want to capture…." *What do I want to capture?*

"It's essence."

Pete smiled. He and this mind-reading pilot would work well together. *As soon as I remember his name.* He pulled his eyes away from the scenery, now feeling like the world was flowing below them—unseen from on high. Turning his head and shifting ever-so-slightly in his bucket-like seat, Pete looked at his pilot. The man simultaneously looked his way for a second, and smiled. It was a charming and simpatico smile. *Yep*, Pete knew for certain, this pilot and he would work together to produce a wonderful and majestic flyover for "Route 66 - Then and Now."

He could even hear imaginary background music. Marilyn LeBue, their Music Supervisor for this film, would most assuredly come up with something classical for his closing flyover scene. She was very good at fitting music type, volume, and placement into her projects. *Yep*, that's why Charlie White had won all those awards. He put together a good team. *Including me.* Pete felt his lips try to move into a smile at his own conceit. But for some reason his face seemed to be stiff—unresponsive. *The wind buffeting my skin because the doors are off?* He'd been forewarned about it being chilly, but not the wind. He'd be sure to ask Jack when back on the ground. *Yep, I'm pretty sure it's "Jack."*

Now psychologically comfortable with a clearer vision on how their film should end, Pete returned his attention outward and below, slightly twisting and turning again. They'd started off from Route 66 flying north, they'd next approached the town of Shiné, where he noted the fireplace and chimney standing seemingly without a house attached. That was a few miles before flying over the town. Then Pete's fancy was caught for a second time. *Is that a castle, on the edge of the town below?* For a moment he felt rather woozy, and wanted to rub his eyes—but quickly realized his hands were occupied holding on to the shoulder straps of the harness keeping him in his seat. *No*, not a real castle, but certainly very castle-like.

Kelso Station would be coming up next he guessed, and he remembered they were scheduled to fly all the way to I-15 before turning back. Pete wasn't sure where the copter's home base was: Jack been picked him up at a rest stop on I-40 while it was still dark, and would be returning him there. By that time

Charlie, Marilyn, and David would have arrived in the Mojave to meet him. *And our new adventure will begin.* Pete again forced himself to relax, take in a long slow breath. Savor the experience, savor the moment.

Because of his noise-reducing headgear, it was surprisingly quiet, so what he heard and saw was an almost silent world gently kissed with the new light of day, and the air he felt on his skin was cool. *Nice.* Indeed, the rising sun was a nearly pure white globe, with broadening bands of saturated yellow emanating—*more like glowing*—from the north and south along the horizon. He blinked, as if what he was experiencing was transitory, and his blink would be similar to a scene cut. But it was real, continuous, and quite amazing how the sunrise could be bright without being blinding, colored without being saturated or intense, and sparkling without being visually confusing. Pete even thought he felt a sun-like warmth on his skin, then immediately laughed at his hyperbolic silliness.

Gorgeous.

As they moved on through the sky, Pete found it hard to remove the stone-chimney and castle-like house out of his mind's eye after he once again took them both in on their return flyover—their iconic shapes even more silhouetted against the remains of the sunrise. He almost sighed aloud with a joy only Pete Lily, *photographer-extraordinaire*, could experience.

"Wonder if anyone is looking up, watching us?" he murmured.

"Doubt it," Jack speculated back. "Looks dead to me."

I know you are officially retired Leiv, but I'm hoping you will reconsider your negative decision this winter regarding nomination to the Illinois Supreme Court. Your name keeps coming up.

Leiv replaced the letter from the Illinois Governor's office in his center desk drawer, and wondered why his old colleague and friend persisted. He was flattered for sure, but it meant rethinking his Shiné life choice—yet again. This particular letter, the latest of three similar missives, had come from a particularly wise old friend, whose counsel he had once relied upon. Leiv had started his library reverie with the letter—but now with a quick decision, pushed the last few inches of the drawer in forcibly enough to cause a snapping sound. With that definitive and dramatic action, he tried to turn his thoughts to HM.

The helicopter intruded upon his morning plans again. This time, unlike earlier, when Leiv was in LC's hexagon glass copula, he didn't have to rely on ethereal-like shadows moving across Shiné Ridge to know the source of the loud motor-type noise. He could see the noisy flying-contraption clearly from his library window. He guessed it was coming back over for a different view, or a second flyover.

His view from his second floor library was not all-encompassing as with the copula, but still moderately panoramic. Especially for enjoying night skies from one of the castle's few non-stained glass windows, where and when it seemed like the stars and moon were quite dramatic, given the solid blackness of Shiné nights. Fleetingly he wondered how often helicopters flew at night, and what it would be like to see one. He hadn't really paid attention since he'd returned to Shiné. *It would probably look like a UFO in the darkness.*

But his mornings were particularly special, and invariably spent either in this room—what he considered his grandfather and father's legacy-room—or up in the cupola as he'd done earlier this morning. Invariably, the question, *library or cupola,* was often his first wide-awake thought. Should he take in the sunrise from the five-sided cupola with its generous windows and window seats at the very top of Rhodes Castle, or from his old-world-comfortable and richly adorned library—the heart, he thought, of LC's monument? Both were spots where Leiv felt he could reach out to his grandfather across the years. Though neither of his "morning spots" had as strong a connection as his grandfather LC's secret cave.

Here in the library, he could touch his father through the furnishings, with their past-century ambiance and multi-generational aspect somehow providing him a link to the past. His grandfather LC started developing "The Library," and left his distinct imprint there; but Leiv was also well aware his father, Everett, built upon that foundation by adding his own enhancements to produce the current "feel" of the place. A feel-of-place that ultimately linked the three generations.

Even this morning, *even* with the draw of the helicopter coming back, Leiv looked fondly at the surrounding floor to ceiling glass-fronted bookcases—now jammed full of legal tomes. He'd shipped much of his Illinois law library to Shiné—some he'd given away, but not a lot. Most he would probably never read again, some, not even open again. *Comfort-possessions*. Books he could feel, touch, smell—and remind him he was the same man who'd sat on the bench in Illinois for so many years. Even though he was now in a different and sometimes alien-feeling spot on planet earth.

Leiv knew the main architectural aspects making both the library and the cupola so special in Rhodes Castle were the large-paned and plain glass windows. Like the one he finally went over to—tracking the helicopter as it moved south and away from Shiné. It was a window quite different from the stained glass ones surrounding the entryway on the floor below, and the ones guarding both sides of the massive fireplace in LC's "withdrawing" room. Indeed, his library window, the one he after a few minutes finally turned away from, was a "real look out and see things" window.

This morning's helicopter appearances—earlier from up high, and this last one from here in the library—were most unexpected. Leiv shivered unknowingly, then shook himself slightly, in similar fashion to earlier in the cupola—but this time with an accompanying shudder-sound.

His thoughts had returned to helicopters for the second

time this morning.

To be fair, helicopters were not a total aerial aberration in Shiné. Occasionally, Bell UH-1Y Hueys—he knew that because Glover told him what kind they were—out of Twenty-Nine Palms Marine Corps Base flew over, heading he didn't know where. He expected Glover knew, but hadn't bothered to pursue more details at the time. But this one, *this* flying-machine looked quite different than the military variety. Bright-blue, sleeker, and smaller.

He had taken a helicopter flight outside of Vegas when first arriving on the West Coast. Smiling, Leiv remembered having to metaphorically pull-up his jaw witnessing the Grand Canyon's grandeur unfolding below him and his fellow passengers. He had also been uncomfortably scared.

"But Shiné's hardly the Grand Canyon," he mused aloud. And *that* helicopter had been quite sizable compared to the one he'd just seen. On this second pass, this morning's helicopter seemed graceful as it curved, even leaned in at an angle it looked like.

His Grand Canyon memory-emotion continued, and this time he felt a shiver go down his back. Leiv was sure his added physical reaction was prompted by re-lived embarrassment. For sure, he had not been an at-ease flyer that morning—tightly grasping some kind of handhold near him. Obviously skittish to anyone who cared to look. *Must have looked like a fool.* Leiv hadn't served in active duty, he had been in the reserves, yet had ridden in a helicopter once before that Grand Canyon tour. He'd hated both experiences.

His fake French antique rotary-phone on the corner of LC's legacy desk rang annoyingly loud—startling Leiv, but fortunately allowing him to escape from memories that still made him cringe. The phone ringing also pulled his attention away from the weird copter intruding upon his Shiné's isolation. Most importantly, the phone's intrusion put a finish to his hoped for morning reverie on what to say and do about Hester Miller.

Leiv also wanted to think over his "should dos" for the upcoming new day. Mornings were a time for introspection and logistics planning. A time he'd come to relish.

Damn phone. In addition, a little accompanying warning-bell was ringing. *Besides, aren't unexpected phone calls ominous by nature?* On a practical level, he further thought, *there must be a way I can turn down that ring-tone.* It would be nice to shift blame for his morning annoyances and building apprehension to the machine itself. *Helicopter's gone, can't fuss at it anymore.*

Actually, Leiv figured Hester would answer by the third ring, and overall he was glad HM—short for "Her Majesty"—screened his telephone life. Nonetheless this time, oddly, inexplicably, and quite contrary to his speculation and HM's gratitude, Leiv reached over and answered the phone himself before it rang again.

"Hello?" He thought he detected HM's telltale click on the other end, and assumed she was eavesdropping as usual.

"Listen," Glover Deers said without preamble or salutation, "I think you're going to want to get down here right away." Chief of Police Glover Deers was his friend and main ally in Shiné. *And most probably my half-brother—*a recent secret and pleasurable piece of deduction he and Glover put together.

Unfortunately, he heard in Glover's normally uncomplicated delivery a mix of urgency and surprise. *Oh no.* "'Down here' is where? Your office?" Leiv hoped it wasn't somewhere out in the desert requiring a long ride, or on somebody's property again. For a second he had to push down lingering unpleasant memories from winter—*motorcycles, dead bodies, Lookout Loop, scrambling for his life on the side of a hill....*

Glover quickly answered his question. "In front of Le Bric-à-Brac. In town."

Mary Jones's place? Alarm bells now rang in full force. "I'm on my way."

Silence on the other end.

He's already hung-up.

11

*   *   *   *   *

Leiv left his second floor library-sanctuary immediately and with regret. Enjoying the morning in his Grandfather LC's and his father Everett's special places this morning was not to be. He sighed heavily as he closed the door behind him. No reason to lock up for privacy, HM could pick any lock in the place.

On his way through the house to his pickup, in passing he grabbed his jacket from the rather rickety antique coat rack at the Castle's massive front entry, then made his way along the first floor corridor. He quickly decided to leave via the kitchen to the garage—*LC's carriage house*—so he could tell HM he was off to town, and give Dobie a quick pat on the head.

Over the last few months his rescued Doberman had chosen HM as his hang-around-with buddy. Of course he knew HM was constantly sneaking the dog liver treats, at least that's what he liked to think was Dobie's reason for choosing kitchen over library. *HM over me.* And he wasn't yet sure if this new Dobie circumstance pleased or depressed him. He wanted Dobie to be happy, but he realized the change was leaving him feeling rather lonely.

When he entered the kitchen, Hester gave him a look of surprise, which he suspected was feigned. Most probably she was listening on the line and knew as much as he did. She asked in one of her more pleasant tones, "If you're going out, should I make you some lunch when you get back?"

"Thanks, but not needed." He figured the lunch offer was a ploy to get him back in the kitchen or dining room as soon as possible so she could pry information out of him. "Don't know when I'll be back." He moved quickly through the kitchen. Dobie was sleeping, so he didn't bother her.

Then from seemingly nowhere, a thought he seldom entertained popped into his mind. *Go easy on HM.* Maybe because she hadn't been her usual vigorously annoying self lately. *Sure hope she isn't sick.* "But thanks for the offer." Leiv hoped his tone was congenial. Then he caught the aroma in the air. "Is that yeast I smell?"

"Yep," she answered.

He smiled, not just at her short and enigmatic-seeming answer, but also because his mind shot back to those days eons ago when his father Everett and his mother Sophie would take him to her mother's house in Austin, in the Chicago area. Grandma Nelson would always have dough rising when they came over. Invariably Sundays, and she had mini-loaf pans—everyone got their own loaf. The food aromas at Grandma Nelson's were all heaven; but the homemade yeast bread in particular. *Special memories.*

She was gone now, but he'd just flown back and visited his mother in her assisted living complex in Oak Park, Illinois a month ago. Shiné to McCarran to O'Hare to Oak Park and back—it had been tiring, but most worth it. He needed to see her, tell her he loved her after his winter adventure. *Things can change in an instant.* She still recognized and remembered him, though once she did call him Everett. Oddly, she couldn't much remember the desert or Shiné. Rhodes Castle, however, she could still verbally walk herself and Leiv through. Her and Everett's actual home, if not its location, was still vibrant in her memories.

"Grandma Nelson made bread." Leiv didn't realize he'd spoken aloud until he heard his own words.

There must have been something in his tone that connected with Hester, for she said, "Grandma Miller made bread, too."

Leiv didn't look back at Hester, but as he crossed the threshold between kitchen and garage and closed the door behind him, he experienced the oddest realization. He and HM had shared a *moment*. A quite new experience for him. And he guessed for her too.

Then from a completely different direction, a vaguely familiar feeling blindsided him. So strongly was he overcome,

Leiv stopped for a moment and swallowed hard. *Something has been started by others again.* Who those others were, he didn't yet have a clue. But instinctively and with a knowing clarity that surprised him—*others* had visions, intentions, and plans he so far knew nothing about. And he would be impacted.

Maybe the helicopter has spooked me, he thought, stepping further out into LC's carriage-house styled garage. *Of course there was also Glover's call.*

"I definitely don't like this," he told the garage as he opened the driver's side door to his dark-blue Ford pickup. Leigh-Everett Rhodes, the former always-in-control Illinois judge, was definitely *not* in control of his world at the moment. Nor was his world a courtroom anymore—his private and tightly controlled bailiwick. Leiv thought he had already come to accept that reality after last year's events in his new Shiné life. Realized his current world was in very few ways comparable to his former life.

Yet here I am, still being taken by surprise.

Another "thing" he was still having trouble swallowing was his fallibility in this Mojave land. He needed to go "talk" to LC in his secret cave as soon as possible. Needed to touch, read, revisit his diary. *Get advice.*

Now however, he was off to talk to Glover—his compass and savior in this generation. Leiv thought a man of his age and experience shouldn't feel so apprehensive. But he did.

Shiné Chief of Police Glover Deers was indeed both surprised and resigned when he called Leiv; but thinking back, he sure hoped those emotions hadn't come through in his call. Though, he guessed they probably had. He'd gotten close enough to Leiv to know he considered Glover the "strong" one. In some ways, Glover figured he probably was—and he couldn't deny he was warming to being Leiv's older brother.

Before calling Leiv, maybe ten minutes earlier—maximum—Glover had just finished tacking up the faxed flyer he'd received from Needles Deputy Sheriff Brad Temper on the cork board above his coffee and tea bar in his modest "break area." Shiné's Chief of Police had most of the latest telecommunication devices available, but not all. Consequently, he appreciated Brad's keeping him posted—even though most items had little relevance to Shiné. Like this one. He posted it anyway. *You never know. Leiv proved that last winter.*

The Police Office was on Main Street, just another plate-glass storefront like the other few businesses in town. It was a modest affair, with a cold-room out back; and in front, two desks, a bench, and a small break area. One desk was kept for whatever public safety personnel might be visiting—like Deputy Brad Temper.

For a second, Glover's mind flitted back to the memory of San Bernardino-stationed Deputy Sheriff Portia Sherman sitting at that desk. Quickly, he banished the picture of her. They'd almost become close last winter, but he doubted there was any real romantic fire there on either of their parts. The desk was just a courtesy spot, *for any public service personal in the area.*

Doc Will Walker and Pastor Lloyd Apply were also known to avail themselves of the spare desk. Glover figured they liked the feel of the reclining swivel-chair. And it pleased him they liked "hanging out" with him occasionally. He'd smiled, and turned away from the cork-board and the picture-poster for Alex—*no last name.*

Then Glover had sat at his own desk for a bit, slouched in his equally padded swivel desk-chair in a most unprofessional manner. His leg stretched out under the desk, and the back of his head rested on his chair's thinly padded upper-back rail.

By then, it was barely minutes *before* Doc Walker called, *before* Pastor Apply called, *before* he actually headed down the street to "Le Bric-à-Brac," and *before* he called Leiv. Glover had also taken a moment to gulp a second cup of coffee while leaving his office, pretty much on the run.

Oddly though, at his office door with his hand on the knob, his stomach jumped a bit, causing Glover to shake his head at the connection between bodily functions and "happenings," as his mother Margaret called them. *Gulped coffee?* He doubted it. Stomach harbingers were one of the bodily functions they both took stock in. *Nope,* this morning he definitely did not like the unfortunately familiar feeling in the pit of his stomach one darned bit. "It" wasn't a sensation he often felt, but when "it" did manifest itself in the past, had been uncannily accurate. He described his personal variety of stomach harbingers once to his mother Margaret as "a feeling similar to the one you get looking over a cliff if you have vertigo." Which he didn't have.

This morning as he usually did, Glover tried to override his emotions, tell himself in no uncertain terms—crime and otherwise inexplicable queasiness are not connected. Realistic as he was though, Glover doubted his mind knew everything he thought it did.

But all that had been *earlier.* Now Walker Johns, Shiné's singular and volunteer ambulance technician, and Doc Walker were both kneeling by the body splayed on Shiné Main Street sidewalk concrete. In front of Mary Jones's place.

Glover knew "this" investigation needed the appearance of being done right. He wanted to sigh, but didn't, and brought his attention to what Doc Walker was saying.

"Trauma to the head..." The Doc's voice sounded surprisingly weak. Like he was a bit queasy, especially for a doctor who looked like the salt-of-the-earth. Glover held back an inappropriate smile. *Puts me in mind of Lionel Barrymore's Dr. Gillespie in the forties.* But Glover knew from experience what the sight of blood from a head trauma did to a person's psyche. Being a doc or a movie star look-alike didn't keep Will from being a human being.

Hopefully, Leiv was on his way. *Damn stomach.*

"It's all about escape and happy endings, now isn't it, Father?" Charlie White looked up into a clear pastel-blue sky. He wanted his words to go directly to his dad, Charles White senior without delay. "I know you can hear me." He smiled, remembering the familiar image of his father in front of the TV watching the 1941 Joel McCrea movie, *Sullivan's Travels.* "You must have seen it a hundred times."

Charlie would never forget how a slice of film, even if only a cartoon section, could bring joy and laughter in a prison scene—*escape.* His father would laugh with the film's characters—sometimes with a hint of a tear in his eye, and not trying to hide his emotion from his son. A father Charlie considered pretty darned sophisticated.

And that's what he wanted in *his* films—escapism, even in a documentary like this one. *Well,* maybe not out and out laughter, but at least a smile of appreciation; a sense of having gone somewhere other than everyday reality. *Escaped* to a land of "happy endings."

"This film starts now, Father," he said before lowering his eyes from the blueness above, which stretched like a protective blanket, it seemed to Charlie, over the vast Mojave Desert vista before him. And, as was a habit of his since film school days at USC, Charlie tapped his forehead with three fingers. He didn't mention the other part of his life, the duplicitous part, figuring his father from wherever his place in eternity was, somehow knew all about that.

They had already picked up his photographer Pete at the I-40 rest stop where Jack was instructed to leave him, and now his full crew awaited in their unmarked Mercedes-Benz film van parked on the shoulder behind him. His cell phone vibrated in his Dockers pants pocket. He pulled it out, saw the number, and didn't answer. "Not now," he said as if his deceased father was still listening. "I have on my 'Producer' hat."

Douglas peered expectantly out his sprinkler-sprayed and dust mottled front window, wondering if he should actually go outside and wait for the filmmaker and his crew. He didn't really know what to expect, and consequently was a bit on edge. A sneeze caught him in mid-thought, and he grabbed for his red bandana-styled handkerchief—fortuitously stuffed in his pants pocket. He was barely in time to catch his sneeze, and consequently concluded it was a wiser move to remain inside. *Cleaner air, don't you think, Hermit?* he rhetorically asked himself.

Dawn had technically come and gone, but it still felt and smelled like early morning, including all too familiar wind-riding desert pollens. Indeed, the "color" of the light also told Douglas what time of year it was—even the time of day. He'd paid attention over the years, and at this stage of his Mojave sojourn, Douglas could almost identify what week of the year it was by assessing the sun, moon, and stars alignment. Then he would add in the clarity and intensity of the light.

Like this morning. If forced, it would be hard to explain to someone else what he called the "feel" of the sun's light. It was more like a picture in his mind, but a picture he "experienced" with his entire body. No calendar needed. This morning was early spring—May to be exact, and one of his favorite times of the year. *Except for these damn allergens.* He swiped his face with his huge handkerchief an additional time before stuffing it back into his coverall work-pants.

His birth certificate read Douglas Chan, the Chan part being picked up generations back, from an ancestor he never knew, and at this point in his life had lost all curiosity about. Once he retired in the Mojave, and settled in as he was on his little hidden-away hill—Shiné locals started calling him "Hermit Chan." Then somewhere along the way, Douglas internalized the name Hermit. Made the moniker his; even when talking to himself. Which he often did.

It's me or the cats. Who else is there to talk to, Hermit? Sure, there was Elizabeth May, and of course he would do anything for the woman; but Douglas knew in his heart, his "love affair" was an unreciprocated old coot's fantasy. Still, he hung on to the idea like a cat with an old favorite play-sock. *A nice thought, though— me and Elizabeth-May.* He wrote a secret song about her when they first met, but never had the courage to sing it to her.

"They should be coming around the last bend soon now," he said aloud to the two unidentifiable-breed cats perched on his inside windowsill. Part of him was excited, but in line with a lifelong predilection toward worrying, Douglas was also apprehensive. The perceptive Jasmine—his dark grey almost black cat—seemed to pick up on his unsettled emotions, and for a moment tilted her head to the side, quizzically peering at him.

Douglas lived with ten cats—part feral, part pet—who stayed mostly inside, but occasionally snuck out and ran about his property. When new ones appeared, he made sure he caught and fixed them all. Still, a couple times a year, a few new ones seemed to appear from nowhere. Fortunately, since he started counting, he hadn't lost any. Indeed, they were smart, with new ones quickly learning the lay-of-the-land. *Inside* were endless treats, soft beds, pillows, play toys, and safety. Definitely better than *outside* where coyotes, owls, hawks, and the like lurked. Elizabeth-May mentioned on several occasions, his cabin, despite its spacious size and lofty design, had the feel of wall-to-wall cats.

With his mind now having returned to Elizabeth-May, doubt crept in to accompany his apprehension. "Maybe I shouldn't have agreed to meet with them?" *Trouble could be stirred up,* he thought, then instantly doubted that would happen. He wasn't about to tell them anything about Elizabeth-May.

Wanting to be left alone was another one of his

propensities. Consequently, the "wise part" of his psyche also told Douglas, it would be good for his mental wellbeing to interact with humans a bit more. *What a talker you used to be, Hermit.* At the same time, his "self awareness" also reminded him, *You've changed a lot since moving to the Mojave.*

After all his pondering, Douglas felt his stomach lurch a bit, and he attempted to re-calm his mind with the mundane thought that at least he wouldn't have to clean up.

His large log cabin, built from a kit when he first moved to the Mojave, and despite the cat population, was always spotless, neat, and fresh-smelling. He kept his desert home just like his city apartment way back when. Immaculate. *Except for the windows here in the Mojave*—impossible to stop sand from blotching them and sliding through the frames. Admittedly, both abodes, then and now, were minimally furnished. *Not a lot of silly knickknacks to attract dust and cat hair.* In lockstep with the inside of Douglas's domain, the close-in land outside—his nectarine trees, a small patch of grass, palms, and a small pond—were all perfectly maintained. The rest of his outside property, like everyone else in Shiné, was a vast expanse of untamed eastern Mojave scrub desert.

Douglas then tried calming his stomach with happy-type thoughts about his upcoming meeting with the filmmaker, Charlie White; not dwell on the possible hazards. For sure, Douglas planned to spin a few yarns about the Shiné startup days—stories he picked up along the way at TGS, the tavern, or at church. Maybe add a few old remembrances from his own earlier Chicago firefighter days. *Film people always seem to want to hear cop and firefighter stories.* Then there was the Route 66 and desert-tale stuff, mostly historical tidbits some old-timers shared with him at TGS's bar. *A lot of them gone now. A lot of my old firefighter buddies gone too.*

He sighed, low, and long—almost with a whistle at the end. This time, both of his window-sitting cats gave him an odd look for a few seconds—and like Jasmine earlier, tilted their heads for a few more seconds before returning to licking their undersides.

"I'll tell them how LC started Shiné for sure," Douglas concluded his train of thought, punctuated with a nod and smile. *At least LC's son Everett and his grandson Leiv's version of events.* But he would definitely keep his mouth shut when it came to Elizabeth-May's property. *Too close for comfort.*

Yet, even after these measured considerations, Hermit's stomach continued to send him warning signals. And quite unexpectedly, his cats jumped down as if they'd been called to an emergency somewhere.

"Well," he said, his audience gone, so now only to himself, "I still think a little excitement is good for the soul. Right, Hermit?" His first fire chief used to quip something similar, but more ribald. Douglas immediately wondered if the sentiment he'd just repeated was truth for him, or just a wishful-thinking pretense—a way of coping. Just like he was sure it was with his chief back then.

Quite a question for you there, Hermit. Was it his stomach *or* his mind pointing toward the truth? He shivered despite the eighty-degree temperature his Koala Bear thermometer suctioned to the inside of his window read. A present from Elizabeth-May. *Tasteless,* he thought, but much treasured.

Maybe I'll go outside and wait.

Mr. Douglas Chan, aka Hermit, was not what Charlie White expected—clean cut in appearance and manner, an average height wiry-looking guy, with intelligent and sharp eyes. *No,* Hermit wasn't the old-geezer "desert rat" he had imagined. His overalls even looked pressed, and Charlie guessed were an affectation.

In addition, on some visceral level, Charlie recognized an aura of formidability emanating from Chan. *Again, a surprise.* This man was capable of doing what needed to be done. It was an odd recognition, but on the mark, Charlie believed. Especially since Chan reminded him of himself—not only in height and build, but also in his public-body-language. *Relevancy?* He wasn't sure. Just another tidbit his brain picked up and would store until needed, then use down the line in some film, someway, somewhere. *Yes, Douglas Hermit Chan, you'll definitely end up a character. Probably a bad'un because of your charming looks.*

When they came around the huge bolder marking what Charlie understood was their final landmark, Douglas waved and called out to them with authority, "Over here." He had meticulously explained beforehand to watch out for the gigantic rock and a small but thick stand of Athol trees.

Now, another surprise—a fancy upscale house. Pete Lily did not mention the cabin in his quickie flyover summary. *Must not have stood out to him. Evidently not catching his artistic eye,* Charlie mused while happily trudging forward. He wasn't a log cabin connoisseur, but he'd directed an episode for a TV special entitled "American Abodes," and consequently recognized Chan's place was upscale and of quality.

Up to this point in their "journey, Charlie was content doing as Chan instructed—not yet feeling bold enough, or comfortable enough in his Mojave and Route 66 surroundings not to. Besides, he had several agendas, and needed to take it slow and easy. *Always a balancing act.* These were the beginning baby-steps forward into the world of his new "Route 66—Then and Now" documentary—*but I also need to keep my mind clear. Be on the watch-out.*

He hoped this man would be a bridge between the history of the area and the present. Invaluable information if his film was to be successful. In addition, up to this point, Charlie had taken care to measure his emotional steps, not acting too eager—not rushing into production or scene-blocking without taking the necessary time to step back for a moment. Think "it" over a second time, and combine his several objectives.

He knew his producer résumé was now solid, including two Emmy and International Documentary Association nominations—partly because he was able to squelch his kid-like excitement enough to put on and maintain his "professional-front" when required. Production leaders needed to be optimistic, excited—but not imbecilic in expressing their eagerness.

Assuredly, he was no longer a neophyte in that emotional balancing-act arena, and knew he was right now at a point where he needed to curb his enthusiasm. *Still a challenge, though.* Charlie anticipated this shoot would again test his "maturity." And now, at last, they were about to meet and talk with Chan. Dealing with this man who he guessed held key information, was his first significant "producer maturity-test" on this film. He dually needed the man's help, and wanted to like him. *Too early for personality conflicts.* Or too many questions. Chan said he didn't encourage trespassers; hence their tedious and complicated uphill approach. *Another clue into the workings of this man. I need to tread lightly.*

In a quick flashback, which prompted a bemused smile, Charlie relived their initial start of this trek up the hill to Hermit Chan's. It had taken his little crew at least fifteen or twenty minutes just to get to their first described starting point—a marker boulder on the dirt road Chan directed them to watch out for from the paved two-lane. Then there was another steep climb up a footpath, again pre-instructed and pre-warned about.

"No vehicles up my road," Hermit Chan's unique and distinctive voice insisted over what Charlie intuited at the time was a landline. Intuited mainly based on the good quality of the connection.

With that guess in mind, Charlie had confirmed his supposition on the way, based on noticing there were very few cell phone towers since leaving I-40; there were however, substantial electric lines along with another spindly swaying line running along the road, and continuing up the path they trudged

23

up minutes earlier. He guessed that was *the* telephone landline.

Remembering in detail, Charlie felt his smile broaden thinking about Hermit Chan's phone choice, but quickly he forced control over his thoughts, reining his bemusement back a notch. There was the sobering fact he might need good communications at some point—and the existing infrastructure might not be up to the challenge. *Out here in no man's land.* So far *their* cells were working. But where are the towers?

Even with these practical concerns about the Mojave, Charlie wasn't successful in pulling his thoughts from their adventure so far. Especially since about halfway up their torturous climb, his cameraman, Pete Lily had said with authority, "Stop." Charlie did as bid without turning around. He'd worked with PL before, and guessed his eye had caught something.

PL was the best Scene-Framer he ever worked with—no exceptions. He was also a prime example of what Charlie had learned early on, and stuck with whenever he could. *Surround yourself with the best and listen when they tell you something.* The rest will come. Peer recognition and a constant demand for Charlie's production, filming, or directing expertise provided solid validation for his working team-maxims—and in particular, his friend PL's abilities. *Actually, the quality of my whole team.*

At Pete's called-for stopping-point on their hike up to Douglas Chan's, he next said, "Look at how the sun is highlighting the ragged ridge way across the valley, north of here." Pete then pointed northeastwardly. Next he held up his hands and made a viewfinder frame with thumbs and index fingers. "Different from earlier. And different from looking down on the horizon this morning from the copter."

The picture framing gesture was one Charlie found annoying and rather silly whenever someone used it; but he knew PL thought it useful, and he didn't chastise or argue with his scene-framer. He turned and looked at the piece of landscape PL was trying to capture—trying to also see what he was talking about. Indeed, the slice of Mojave terrain and daylight PL referred to was quite spectacular.

Charlie hadn't realized there were hill peaks and drops like that out there. But the angle and position of the sunlight was highlighting the depth of the ridge's cragginess. "Nice." He knew PL didn't require long-winded statements of appreciation. "No matter where else we end up shooting, we need to use that ridge in a shot, don't you think?"

"Yep," PL agreed.

But Charlie didn't like the thought of scrambling around those ridges. Even driving them didn't appeal to him. Ironic he knew, in that he had done far more strenuous and treacherous activities in the past. "Maybe the closing shot," he added, his artistic senses moving forward to filming sequence, and further leading his mind ahead to his ending scene. *Dad would love that ridge.* "I wonder if that ridge has a name?" When he looked for a second time, and more closely, the ins-and-outs of the ridge PL highlighted really were rather dramatic.

"Yes, for closing," Pete agreed. "And I've already got a lens in mind that's perfect for handling a sweeping aerial shot like that while simultaneously catching the terrain details."

The look on PL's face said he was now caught up in his photographic-world, so Charlie didn't question him further. *Too early for those kind of decisions anyway.*

Trudging up the path closely behind him and Pete, Marilyn LeBue, his Music Supervisor said, "I can just hear a baroque fugue accompanying a sequence — "

"Don't see anything special about a half-assed sunrise over a pile of low level, less-than-spectacular monotone grey hills in the middle of a God-awful desert," David Milhouse, their set designer grumbled as he brought up the rear. Despite the facts he always gave the impression of being in perfect physical fitness, and the coolness of the morning, beads of sweat were starting to glisten across David's movie-star-perfect forehead. "And the name on the map is Lookout Loop."

"No, Lookout Loop, is over there," Pete said, pointing to the east. "I don't remember the one I'm framing."

David made a sucking sound through his teeth before mumbling in a disgruntled tone, "Look all the same to me."

Funny Davey would confuse the two areas. Not that he couldn't make a mistake, but Charlie doubted he had. *Davey usually has a reason for everything.* And Charlie had seen both Davey and Pete checking out the map together in the backseat. He further thought, *what would I do without Dave?* He almost sighed, but caught himself before anyone on his team would notice.

When it came to films, Davey's knowledge-base usually included geography, but his strength and preference was putting together the ideal set for an English drawing room. Charlie wanted to let his bemusement with those facts morph into a smile. *An English drawing room out here in the Mojave?*

In addition, besides personally liking Davey, when it came to the filming aspect of their relationship, Charlie needed his professional eye for scaling down and making the grandiose manageable—especially on this project, given the breadth of the Mojave desert and Route 66. *Chicago to California. No easy task.* And he was also counting on Davey's knowledge as far as the film was concerned when they actually got to the end of this shoot—Chi-Town. Davey's hometown to boot.

Where they were at the moment wasn't even on Route 66 precisely, and in Davey's world, there might not be any sets per se to design out here in the desert, but his perspective would still be invaluable. They had a lot of traveling still ahead of them, and Charlie wanted it all to be productive. Davey would see to that. For to Charlie's reckoning, in the past, Davey's instincts had been "spot-on" to use a phrase Davey himself was fond of. Truth was, Davey could easily be the most valuable member of the team he assembled—for this shoot and otherwise. His Set Designer was the one person in their little group who didn't see the world through rose-colored, orchestrated, or fanciful fictional filters. He was the realist, with few internal narrative biases Charlie knew of. And in his "all knowing" gut, Charlie intuited a "footing in reality" would end up being crucial to this, his latest adventure. *Adventures*, actually.

There were also logistics to think about. Davey was their procurement guy. When facilities were available, he picked the restaurant, or engaged the Craft Services on-set caterer. In places and shoots like this, however, it would be a matter of knowing where the closest grocery store was, and stocking up on goodies that fitted their van's minimal camping facilities. Although, PL's helicopter pilot, Jack, told them TGS in town had an excellent chef—whose name was also Jack. Pilot Jack, additionally explained TGS was short for The Greasy Spoon.

They trudged on, but not much farther up the hill, and similar to what PL had done earlier, Charlie also stopped, turned toward his team, and stood for a moment, facing them, their silhouettes outlined by the rising sun behind them. "Awesome," he said, swallowing down a lump rising in his throat. Didn't happen with him often, but when it did, quite motivating.

"I know," PL said.

"Indeed," Marilyn agreed.

Davey said, "Seen one sunset, seen 'em all."

"It's a sunrise." PL sounded peeved, though Charlie knew he wasn't and the "sunset" quip was more of a tease than censure.

Once their trek up was completed, and when finally standing on the threshold of meeting Hermit Chan—in Charlie's mind, the real beginning of his new film—he took a deep calming breath before heading forward. Thus, with his crew bringing up the rear, Charlie finally approached Chan's cabin; where a trail of whitish smoke pluming out of a rooftop smokestack caught his eye—and he found it harder than expected to hold back his building emotions again. Admittedly, they were now accompanied by a wee-bit of trepidation.

It was always that way in the beginning of a project. *So let*

27

the adventure begin, he thought, and overtaken though he didn't want to be, Charlie could no longer hold back the quickening of his footsteps—childish or not, anxious or not. They were actually going to interview Chan, the man who would introduce them to the world of Shiné.

Then something else unexpected happened—upon sight of Chan standing in front of his doorway—out of the blue, Charlie's stomach suddenly felt a bit queasy, and he didn't know why. *Trepidation, sure.* But queasiness, not his style. Not in his businesses. *Excitement, yes,* but accompanied with nausea, not so much. Especially since as he and his team continued forward, they were being greeted enthusiastically by the rather dapper Douglas Hermit Chan.

A premonition? He almost said the fanciful and unfamiliar word aloud. Foretelling was not his usual either. Unconsciously, and barely noticeable to even himself, Charlie shook himself.

After many minutes dedicated to niceties—which included greeting and petting what seemed like an endless procession of cats—Hermit once again surprised Charlie with his congenial and polished hosting skills. Finally, after all the cat rubbing rituals by humans and felines, it didn't then take long before Charlie and his crew were all sitting on comfy tufted-leather couches grouped in the center of what Hermit dubbed his "great room."

Nice open feeling, Charlie thought. *Douglas Hermit Chan surprises just keep coming.*

Before Douglas officially joined the little party himself, he offered, "Can I pour some 'Gentleman Jack' whiskey?"

"It's eight in the morning." PL sounded incredulous but quite pleased. "Of course I was up at dawn flying in a copter...." Charlie knew from experience PL could drink anytime booze was available. But he also heard Marilyn and Davey both say with more anticipation than he would ever have guessed, "Yes, please."

Charlie shook his head and passed on the Gentleman Jack—but marveled. *Amazing. breakfast booze*—with his photographer, music-maven, and realist all willing to down shots at eight in the morning.

As Hermit poured—dispensing liquor from what looked like a crystal decanter—retrieved from a rough-hewn sidebar, Charlie was struck by the clash in styles and periods between decanter and sidebar. Davey was a stickler for set-continuity, and some of it had rubbed off on him. Nonetheless, clashing periods aside, Charlie mainly marveled in a different direction. *This is a comfortable house. And Douglas Hermit Chan is definitely a remarkable man.* A realization prompting further wonderment and question as to how many new surprises the Mojave would be conjuring up for him this shoot. *More complications to an already complicated endeavor.*

His train-of-thought was cut short by Hermit handing him a half full cut-glass crystal whiskey-tumbler—*despite* his just declining his offer.

But *before* he could object without impolitely pushing the surprisingly heavy glass back directly into the old man's hand, Douglas somehow managed to sit down next to him, and *before* Charlie could utter any words of objection or set his glass down, his host asked quite directly, "Why are you making this movie?"

To please my dead dad, Charlie thought without reflection. To Douglas, he answered after half a moment or so, "Route Sixty-Six and the desert are popular these days." It was a true statement, Charlie knew, but a look of incredulity spread across Douglas's face. A look so outrageously clear, it almost caused Charlie to laugh at himself. *Knows I'm feeding him half-truth pabulum.*

Despite the look on his face, "Hmm," was all Douglas actually said.

Something about that look also told him Chan knew more

than he was going to be telling them this morning. Hopefully, he would "share" a more personal conversation sometime later. Charlie's instincts told him, now was not the time. Indeed, he imagined them sitting down together again, down the road a bit. Tumblers once again full of Gentleman Jack to loosen both their sets of lips—and hopefully at a little more appropriate time of day. *Though I do like this man who drinks whiskey at eight in the morning.*

"Who owns that burnt-out house with only a chimney and fireplace left standing?" Pete asked from the rocker across the room. Charlie noticed Pete's whiskey tumbler was now empty. So was Marilyn's. David was sitting in an armchair to his right, and he couldn't see him or the status of his whiskey tumbler without being obvious. For his own part, Charlie unobtrusively, he hoped, set his still-full tumbler on the side table next to him.

"A chimney?" Hermit answered by way of a question couched in what Charlie guessed was a fake innocent expression.

"Looked like it wasn't too far from here," Pete added, uncertainty in his tone.

Douglas tilted his head as if thinking, then tsked out the side of his mouth. "Hmm." Then he tsked again. "Can't help you there."

Clearly, Hermit Chan had no intention of helping them on the location of the chimney. *Curious,* Charlie thought. And his stomach twitched again. *Maybe I should have a slug of that whiskey.* His dad had thought booze was medicinal on many fronts.

Leiv was surprised Glover was standing on the sidewalk alone when he arrived at Le Bric-à-Brac on Main in Shiné. He parked quickly, bent over and slipped under a strip of yellow police tape connected to a light post on one end, and on the other end tied to a dumpster in the alley next to one of six empty storefronts in Shiné. He walked over to stand next to Glover. Greetings weren't exchanged. *We know all too well why we're here.*

Leiv felt his body stiffen, and his legs automatically take a solid and slightly wide-legged stance. He knew his physical "handling" of the circumstances wasn't in his control—so he tried to ignore his reflexes for the moment.

A body was covered with a green and red tartan patterned tarp. The whole area was squared-off by more police tape running from the lamppost at the street corner, all the way down the sidewalk in front of the antiques store, cordoning off completely the east side of Main in front of Le Bric-à-Brac.

Hardly necessary in that no curious locals were milling around anywhere. *Most people in Shiné stay home. Which is where I'd rather be.* Leiv quickly corrected himself aloud by saying to Glover, "Thanks for calling me." Truth was, and he had no idea why, he felt a tinge of excitement somewhere in his gut—despite his growing inclination over the last couple years to become more of a recluse—especially after the unpleasant events this last winter. *Some piece of kid buried in my psyche must want to go on another adventure with Glover.*

In addition, whatever was going on here, Mary Jones was involved, and Leiv knew he was quite fond of her; consequently, he needed to help her if he could. Then quite unexpected, but only for a few seconds, an intense nausea, accompanied by a quite different feeling in the pit of his stomach he wasn't familiar with grabbed at his gut wiping out any adventure-excitement he thought he might be experiencing. Fortunately, as quick as the nausea and queerness came, in a few more seconds—they were gone. But his longing for excitement did not also return.

He took a mental deep breath, calming himself. It was still fairly early, a slight wind was warm, and the scent of spring freshness was floating on the air currents. *Nice.* And fortunately he'd worn a jacket over his chambray shirt. But the dead body at his feet marred any moments of morning-niceness he might wish for. *No,* he was about to take in a dead body. Leiv cursed mentally.

"You want to see the body?"

As ready as he could be, Leiv nodded. During his years as a judge, he'd unfortunately viewed a couple bodies, but nothing like what a cop was used to dealing with. Leiv *thought* he certainly didn't want to see *this* body, yet he knew he had to and followed Glover the few steps to the edge of the tarp. He took another breath, this one physically deep, long, and fortifying, he hoped. "The shroud isn't what I would expect." He was thinking it should be a solid color, like yellow or blue. *Funny the things that pop into your head at times of stress.*

"It's a tarp," Glover said. "Not a shroud." His tone was teasing, not derisive. "You are fanciful sometimes. We do also have a body bag, but I can't do that crappy body-bagging routine until the forensic technician coming from Needles gets here. And they might call in a full forensics unit from San Bernardino from the Scientific Investigations Division."

"Why the formalities?" Wasn't Doc Walker, who doubled as Shiné's emergency coroner good enough?

By way of answer, Glover squatted, grabbed the corner of the tartan-tarp and pulled it back enough for Leiv to see the victim's face. "You recognize him?"

Indeed he did. *Johnny Max.* He was the actor kicked off a long running soap opera because of very public bar fights, several DUI charges, and the last incident Leiv remembered— punching a director on set. Leiv didn't actually follow "soaps," but he'd stood in enough grocery lines to see Johnny Max's wild-eyed face, and read the sixty-point plus headlines. *Hard to miss.* In addition, and for some reason he would never fathom, HM and Margaret Deers followed the show almost religiously and occasionally discussed juicy tidbits in his presence.

Leiv figured some of Max's high jinks were for publicity purposes, but punching your director, he thought, was over the top. Indeed, before leaving the show, his antics were not only fodder for tabloid outlets, but started getting mentions on network and cable TV channels. Police were involved a couple times, but victims never pressed charges. He'd wondered, only once and briefly, if Max was being protected somehow. *More like protecting their money interest,* he now thought looking upon the dead man's face. "Too bad," he said, even though Glover wouldn't know where his mind had been.

Now Johnny Max was dead, lying face-up with a halo of dry sticky-looking fluid on the concrete around his head — *blood of course* — causing him to look like a perverted caricature of a pretty-faced fallen angel. Leiv sighed loudly — and it wasn't only because of his thoughts, or sadness accompanying experiencing anyone's dead body on the sidewalk; but also because he knew more about Mary Jones than most. And it was his duty to tell Glover. Nonetheless, he debated a long moment before actually speaking. Being a judge for so many years, and his accompanying respect for the law overrode his fondness and protectiveness toward Mary Jones, though. He doubted Mary confided in Glover like she had with him, so it was up to him to provide the information Glover needed to know.

After Glover lowered the tarp — which Leiv still thought of as a shroud, he said somberly. "I need to tell you something about Mary and this man."

"That he's her ex?" Glover's voice was flat — no emotional spin.

So Mary's secret wasn't so secret after all. Leiv shook his head, sighed again, *this time* barely audible, and *this time* at his own naiveté. "I thought I was the only one in town who knew who she was." *I thought I was her special confident.* "Hubris on my part looks like."

"She's an interesting woman," Glover said enigmatically, and again with no emotional spin.

"Where is she?"

"Upstairs." Glover didn't look up toward the second floor of Le Bric-à-Brac.

Leiv did, half-expecting Mary to be looking down at

them. Maybe giving them a friendly wave. "Damn."

Glover echoed him with, "You can say that again." After a moment, he added. "Brad's on his way. The Bus will follow like I said before—forensic and medical techs. I've asked him to do the official interview, and for them to give Mary a medical once-over." Now sadness clearly edged Glover's tone. "She's upstairs. I talked to her when I first got here. A little off in her reactions. Her speech was slightly slurred, and she kept rubbing her eyes like there was something she didn't want to see. At one point I thought I'd have to hold her up, but she waved me off and sat down. She says she's okay. Doesn't want medical attention, but she's going to have a medical evaluation whether she wants it or not." Silence fell for a couple moments, before Glover concluded, "From what I can see, Johnny Max took a header off her balcony."

Leiv's voice was almost a whisper. "So our Mary is the obvious suspect?"

"Yep."

"That's why you want Brad to interview her?"

"Yep." Glover turned to Leiv. "I don't want it to be her. I want there to be some kind of accident explanation." He blew out a long resigned-sounding breath. "And I'm too close."

"I understand." He still retained defense-argument memories for several defendants he'd so wanted to be innocent. "I'm feeling the same." *But I'm not the Chief of Police.* "You think the County will charge her?"

Glover shook his head. "Probably only if I recommend it." Then Leiv waited patiently as Shiné's Chief of Police took a full-fledged deep breath this time—slowly in and out—*then* puffed up his cheeks, *then* took another, but releasing his intake of air even more slowly than the previous one. He was in uniform, his regular light blue shirt, dark pants, and had been holding his three-inch brimmed 'Smokey the Bear' campaign hat woodenly in front of him. Now he quite deliberately put it back on with an edge of formality. "Brad can have a heavy-foot when he wants to.

Should be here soon."

"Are you going back up?" Leiv asked.

"Like I said, I'm waiting for Brad."

"Shouldn't she be in custody, or with someone, or something?" Leiv imagined Mary upstairs, alone and distraught. "She's all alone."

"This isn't a TV show," Glover said. "You want me to deputize you so you can go hold her hand?"

"Yes."

Glover laughed, breaking their somber mood for a few seconds. "I already called my mother. She's on her way here to sit with her. 'Hold her hand.'"

"Can I go in the shop?" Leiv wasn't sure why he was acting like a besotted teenager. But he was. Another one of those changing personality things he would think about later. But right now, all he wanted to do was go into Le Bric-à-Brac and connect with Mary.

"You can go in the shop if you have to." Glover sounded like he was talking to a child.

Probably with just cause.

"But don't touch anything," Glover further admonished.

Again, *probably with just cause.*

Glover would never forget his Police Academy and FBI SWAT training classes. Prime duty and first objective was to secure the scene. *And here I stand, in the middle of Shiné's Main Street, securing a scene with no crowd to control, no "street evidence" to keep in place, no hoards of fellow cops tromping all over doing their assigned tasks.*

Shiné was a different world. Some would even perceive Shiné as a ghost town. They would be wrong. *Sure a lot of store fronts are empty.* He knew though, there were many real people who lived in Shiné. And even though he was the Police Chief, these people were becoming a family to him. Not just his mother Margaret whom he moved back to California to be with—his feeling of family was broadening. He hadn't really thought about it much in the past, this familial thing. Considering this insight, Glover speculated that might be the reason for his attachment to Mary Jones. *A feeling of family? Or could it be romantic attraction?* Neither were emotions he was free to indulge in when it came to law-enforcement and suspects.

He mentally paused, and listened for a second. Usually Glover could hear birds chirping as they rushed from electric poles and phone posts around Shiné. He fancied they were in town resting from their forays out into the openness surrounding a Shiné oasis. This morning, nothing. Dead quiet.

Recently, only a couple months back, he went to a Force Continuum class on what to do when confronting a suspect— announcing his presence, then giving commands before actual contact of any kind. Glover almost laughed aloud thinking about his current suspect, Mary Jones, sitting and waiting in her apartment atop Le Bric-à-Brac this deathly quiet, rather surreal morning on Shiné's Main Street. Not a scene contemplated in that class for sure.

From the moment he received a call from Doc Walker, who had received a call from Chef Jack who came into town in the wee hours to get everything set up for opening TGS, and then another call from Walker Johns, Shiné's volunteer ambulance driver and sometime deputy stand-in—Glover *knew* Mary had killed her husband. Who else could it be? She was guilty of murder for sure. With that easily arrived-at conclusion, he also intuitively started thinking about Leiv. *If I figured it out so fast...Leiv is smarter than I am, he'll know, too. And fast.*

"Damn," he whispered to a Main Street, empty except for him and Johnny Max's dead body.

* * * * *

Once inside Le Bric-à-Brac's first floor showroom, Leiv was compelled to turn around and look back outside through the shop's unique door windows at Glover. He was still standing on the same spot of Shiné sidewalk where he had left him just a moment earlier. A passage from LC's journal pushed itself forward into Leiv's consciousness, *"...a church, a tavern, and sidewalks make a town. Viola will prevail with the church and sidewalks...but I'm thinking...the tavern is up to me."* Indeed, Chief of Police Grover Deers—his friend, Margaret Deers and his father Everett's "secret" child, *my older brother on my grandfather's side*— was still standing rigidly on Viola's sidewalk. And like so many things this last year, there was a significance there Leiv would have ignored a couple years earlier, but no longer could. A connection to a past he wasn't sure he was eager, or yet able to make.

Leiv wanted to explore whatever the significance was of "Viola's sidewalks" in the hodge-podge of mental and physical assimilations he'd been forced to experience the last couple years; but before he could blink, more recent memories replaced LC's journal thoughts.

An uncanny familiarity caused him to turn from the front window for a moment and step forward farther into Le Bric-à-Brac proper, once again finding the spot Mary showed him inside her shop last winter. *"If you stand in just the right place, and look through the curve of the front window at just the correct angle..."* And just like with that moment last winter, he saw the non-happenings on Main Street, all the way down to TGS. Even this morning, despite a dead body lying on the sidewalk, and Glover standing on guard—it was the same.

Eerie I can remember the exact spot in her shop, Leiv thought. Then he rubbed his forehead. Not so much because he was reliving a past moment in such vivid detail, nor the reality there never seemed to be a crowd milling around on Main Street— *Viola's sidewalks,* but more because an overall twilight zone impression suddenly descended upon him out of nowhere. The experience was so complete, it was as if any second, the appropriate Twilight Zone TV show intro-music would start playing.

Unacceptable thoughts for a former judge. Leiv rubbed his head even harder—on both sides, with both hands. Wasn't he just revisiting an offer from the Illinois Governor's office this morning? Asking if he was interested in an appointment to the Illinois Superior Court? And here he was in an antique-curios shop of sorts, in California's Mojave desert, hundreds of miles from a decent-sized city—thinking and acting like a fanciful loony-tunes.

Ironic. He'd seen more than his share of "thinkers" who lived in alternate-universes in his court room. *Now I've become one.*

He pulled himself away from looking at Glover and "feeling" Shiné, and tried to rein in his imagination. He needed to take in Le Bric-à-Brac on a real-time basis—on this morning of a homicide. A homicide in Mary Jones's world, not his off-kilter imagination, nor the contrivances of Hollywood soap opera directors. A very dead Johnny Max was lying on the pavement, and Mary Jones waited upstairs. *What an awful morning.*

"Your fault," he said into the silent shop, referring to his runaway imagination, and addressing his grandfather LC across the years. The more he read of LCs diary, and re-read sections even for a second and third time—Leiv marveled at the whimsy of the man. Especially since he had mainly thought of LC as a hard pioneer type. In his mind, to have done what LC did, in the circumstances surrounding him, and with the available US Western infrastructure available a the time—took a strong, hard man. Nonetheless, Leiv had found revealing tidbits in LC's diary that showed more in his grandfather's personality than just grit and determination.

"I don't have your grit, but clearly, I have your whimsy." There was no echo to his words spoken into Mary's empty antiques showroom. In fact, his proclamation seemed to float away on an unseen current in the showroom—disbursing his thoughts with them.

His mind once more took him back in time as he remembered Mary—dressed in her flowing antique dress, no makeup to giveaway she was a TV star, her dark eyes nonetheless sparkling, lifting the little crater-pocked blue bottle into the air that strange day last year. A bottle that ended up being crucial to solving Naomi Hall's death. Even now, and only as a memory playing in his brain, his experience remained a strikingly memorable moment.

Leiv wiggled his shoulders in lieu of an all-out shudder from reliving that day's emotion so vividly. He turned back to the door, half expecting a stream of sunlight finding its way from her storefront glass window to touch the little bottle. Just like it had that morning. Of course, there was no bottle this morning in an aberrant stream of sunlight; but still, Mary's words of explanation came back, *"It's a Hobnail Penny perfume bottle, I think..."*

He was finding it hard to pull himself away from that day with Mary. *Maybe it's this shop that makes me crazy.* Because even last year, it was a quite unique and other-worldly experience as they both touched the Hobnail Penny perfume bottle.

Leiv thought further and decided, *no,* it's not Le Bric-à-Brac. Not the place. *It's Mary Jones.* The woman herself. Even Glover said she was interesting. *Way more than that for me.* Leiv took a deep breath, straightened his shoulders, and looked over toward the doorway in the back of the shop. A door he suspected led to Mary's upstairs apartment. It was closed.

Well, he wasn't a judge anymore, so she certainly wasn't about to appear before him in court. And unless Glover was charging and taking her in, Leiv decided he was going to go upstairs and talk to her.

Hell with Glover anyway; Shiné's Chief of Police would just have to fuss at him afterwards. Besides, and contra to his straightforward reasoning thoughts, a little voice in the back of his head was whispering, *going upstairs is just what Glover wants you to do.*

Elizabeth-May thought she saw a smallish white car come down the road toward her turnoff, but didn't see it continuing on past down the road heading north. Admittedly, her eyesight was getting more wobbly with age, and at the time she noticed its appearance, her mind and emotions were only partly occupied by the vehicle. She wasn't particularly worried anyway, the auto-disappearing phenomena had happened many times in the past. It was how the curve bent, and that annoying stand of Athols obstructing her line-of-sight view on the north end of the road. Of course she didn't have the heart to cut the trees down, and her several attempts at pruning had only made them thicker.

Carrying her train of thought further, she lamented aloud, "And folks drive faster than my reflexes these days." She tapped her front picture window to the world with the index and middle fingernails of her right hand, as if admonishing the car and driver—while simultaneously stroking Tempe's head with her left hand. Tempe was a larger than average German Shepherd mix, "the mix" part being unknown. He was her soul mate, and as was his habit when she looked out her window to the world, he sat at her side and did the same. She also shared many of her thoughts with him, and from experience, Elizabeth-May knew his eyes were intense, clearly transmitting his canine intention to make sure her concerns and safety were addressed. *I'm so lucky,* she often thanked God for Tempe. He was the smartest and most intuitive dog she ever had.

This was the second house Elizabeth-May lived in on this piece of property, and her second window to the world. The first house she experienced as a child, and with a child's-eye view. That house was expanded upon by her parents, Jules Junior and Elizabeth Senior, with help from her grandparents, Jules Senior and Anna Logan who built her first home. Root cellar and chimney included—ice was hard to come by back then.

Sadly but also gratefully, her mother wasn't around to see the original homestead burn down. *Nothing but that chimney left.* For a few seconds, she allowed her mind to flitter-around with memories of her mother. Then of Tony, her deceased husband, and how he'd helped her rebuild. Quickly though, her thoughts returned to her dad. She retained so many memories from watching her father add on to her grandparent's home. Of course her mother was there helping. Picking out the new stones that matched, laying them one by one with care. With love even, Elizabeth-May thought later in life.

It was a very good thing Tony did, helping me rebuild once more—put this house up. Even using railroad ties and stones like her parents and grandparents had done on the original house. *He helped me restore my memories.*

"Cost a pretty penny, it did." In a little spot of her down-to-earth thinking mind, there was a tiny place reserved for magical-thinking that allowed Elizabeth-May to believe Tempe often understood what she was telling him.

She touched her expansive picture window again, this time with the flesh of her fingertips, gently, almost lovingly. It was warm, and that surprised her. Unusual, especially given the time of the day, and in her past experience no matter the season, *this glass* usually felt cool. She couldn't actually see her own reflection, the light was not right to send her image back to her— but in line with her magical-thinking musing, Elizabeth-May fancied she could see herself and Tempe.

Unfortunately, apprehension she knew was waiting in the wings, wanted to take over. Elizabeth-May could feel it slyly sending tentacles through her being, and she saw that concern reflected back in her own mirrored-eyes. She even *fancied* an apparition was wagging a finger at her from the glass, reminding her, cautioning her—the inevitable was near.

"But you can't relive your life, undo what's been done."

41

She sighed the sigh of wisdom gained from living a long life. "What's done is done," she repeated. Consciously and with determination, she pulled her hands away from the window, then smoothed the front of her girlish pink dress—much like her hands were a symbolic iron. Elizabeth-May thought her frilly selections never seemed to iron correctly. She was a tall, large-boned thin woman, and thought her large featured face didn't exude much feminine charm or allure. Consequently, her frilly wardrobe—adopted way-back as a teenager. She always wished she looked like Katherine Hepburn—but knew in her heart she didn't.

As Elizabeth-May continued to look out into her world, an inquisitive ray of light touched a rusting piece of metal somewhere on the aged school bus, parked behind the huge Ash tree her mother had planted many years ago. *"Not suited for here,"* her father had complained. But it had thrived, now protecting a rusted-out 70s-era mini school bus beneath its now expansive boughs and massive trunk. Several collectors had offered her money for the bus—but she'd passed. Ironically, she considered the Ash far more valuable.

"Well, Tempe," she asked her canine friend as he looked up at her on cue. It was that time of day. "Shall we go make a cup of tea and take those miniature cupcakes out of the freezer and some bisquits for you?" Elizabeth-May fancied he nodded—though she knew it was more like a yawn.

For sure, there was no point sitting around fretting, waiting for the inevitable. Margaret Deers and Mary Jones were coming over for their monthly book club brunch meeting Monday. She needed to straighten up a bit today and tomorrow, make some cookies maybe? *No*, a cake. The remaining cupcakes would not be enough. A little sigh she didn't notice escaped. Admittedly, their gathering was not quite the same since losing Naomi, Georgie, and Ida. But they still enjoyed their monthly "event," as Margaret called it.

"I bet even you didn't guess Ida was a cold-blooded killer

last winter?" she teased Tempe.

Her canine companion shook his head, which caused her to smile, even though Elizabeth-May knew for sure this time it was because his ears itched. She would have to put some more medicine in both ears. *Ear mites probably.*

Still, despite her philosophical resignation, and the enjoyment she received from communicating with her best friend and soul mate, Elizabeth-May knew *it had started.* Indeed, her stomach was starting to feel a bit queasy. *A harbinger? Yes,* Elizabeth-May was sure it was.

Looks like she's alone, Mugs concluded. He'd found an Athol-sheltered spot to the north of Elizabeth-May's house. It was a blind spot of sorts, no windows out that side of the house. He caught himself rubbing his mouth and chin with the slender long-fingers of his left hand — then willed his hand to his side. No time for nervous habits. *I need to pay attention to what I'm doing.* He was a man of discipline. *Have to be, to do what I do.*

The house he was looking at wasn't exactly modest — but it wasn't fancy either. Looked like railroad ties were used in some of the overhangs, but he wasn't sure if he knew what a railroad tie actually should look like. *Just a guess.* But railroad ties or not, Anthony L's place was definitely a surprise. Not because of the rustic style, but because he'd expected him to have lived higher-on-the-hog than this place. *Have more of a flashy kind of place. Hell, Anthony L made a lot of money in "the day."*

Mugs knew for certain Anthony L. was a snappy dresser; so this place and the man he had known just didn't fit. At the very least he expected a house more like that castle he spied further down the road before he turned around — closer-in to that podunk town with the funny name. He couldn't quite remember it at the moment, but he knew it was just one word.

He shook his head in disgust, but also with a touch of

wonderment at this alien world. He decided he needed to wait a bit, take in the "lay of the land" so to speak. But his mind wouldn't yet let go of Anthony L's choice of "retirement" spot. *Why would Anthony L want to live out here?* He guessed there wasn't even a gym to work out in. Not that he expected there would be one in the desert. *I'm not that stupid.* Another item Mugs was proud of, his well-toned body, especially for a man of his age.

Mugs considered anew whether he should go in right away, overpower the old broad, make her hand it over. Get this job done, then move on to Johnny Max. To that end, he pulled a picture out of what he fondly called his "fixer-bag." The snapshot was supposedly recent, and showed what he guessed to be an eighty-something woman, dressed in an ugly frilly dress that went back decades, and long circle earrings.

Mugs shook his head yet again. *Can't account for love.* Even he knew that—but how Anthony L could have fallen for this woman in this god-awful place was a real head-scratcher.

As a result of his considerations, he decided anew. He should go in now. Wouldn't take long—in and out. But then he heard a car motor. *Not now.* Nonetheless, professional that he was, Mugs pulled his emotions back, let his adrenalin level subside, and waited until the car came into view on the front main driveway to Anthony L's place. Soon he could see it was a van.

A van? Didn't make sense. Mugs made a sucking sound, louder than he should have, and upon hearing himself, tsked more softly through his teeth. Then out of nowhere, Mugs felt a flash of unfamiliar nausea, which quickly passed. *I don't get quesy.* This time Mugs allowed himself a derisive and whispered little chuckle. *Especially not in the line of work I'm in.* Nonetheless, Mugs knew his stomach was telling him—something *he* hadn't planned for had started. He didn't like that one bit. Up to now, his success had ridden on planning, cool-headedness, and being prepared. No surprises. A tinge of unwanted apprehension tried to re-assert itself. But Mugs Nightshade was not a man easily riled. *Nothing to worry about.*

"I hope you don't mind me intruding," Leiv called out.

He knocked, then rang the buzzer next to the door, but didn't receive an answer of any kind. So Leiv boldly tried the door, and when it opened, walked up the one flight of stairs to find Mary Jones standing in front of an unlit antique cast-iron fireplace—her back to him, and seemingly staring down into a nonexistent fire.

Mary didn't move, so he guessed she hadn't heard him call out, and he didn't want to scare her—so he coughed. Loudly. And he heard her laugh as she quickly turned to face him with a smile on her face despite the circumstances.

"Always the gentleman," she said, her eyes saying she was glad to see him. Nonetheless, she didn't move forward. "I'm so glad you've come to see me before—"

"It won't be Glover. But Deputy Sheriff Brad Temper from Needles."

"Of course." Her smile remained. "Come and sit down, we can talk a bit."

Mary was as he remembered her from the last time they met, dressed in her usual layered antique dresses—a Shiné disguise of sorts he guessed. That meeting was a chance encounter at Shiné's Pump and Fill next to TGS about a month earlier. They had waved, she'd blown him a kiss, and he almost walked over to her pumping island to invite her to one of his Saturday night *soirees*, as Pastor Apply sometimes called their friends gathering. But he didn't. *Scared to,* he thought at the time. Later, he came up with the rationalization he'd filled his tank already, no reason to hang around. He could easily ask her anytime. Maybe even make a point of stopping in at her shop.

After all, his get-togethers at Rhodes Castle weren't

anything special, just a weekly gathering of the few folks he'd become attached to in Shiné. Pastor Apply, Margaret Deers, and recently Margaret's son, Police Chief Glover Deers. It was also a nice way of sharing LC's "withdrawing" room, and his legacy. A few aperitifs, a little finger food chosen and prepared by HM. And of course, congenial conversation. There was plenty of room to expand the gathering. Yet, he'd hesitated.

Leiv knew there was much more involved in his not inviting her at that time, and he wasn't sure what it was—hence his excuses. A feeling he would be taking a step forward in a yet unknown journey involving her? *No, too fanciful.* Whatever his fear at Shiné's Pump-and-Fill back then, it was evidently still with him and maybe controlling him this very morning. *More than just a feeling—a prohibition almost?* But why? *I really like her.*

He was quite experienced in dealing with contradictory and inexplicable emotions and thoughts. *In others.* It was familiar ground, having to navigate through verbiage and documents from DA's, *usually their assistants*, defense attorneys, defendants, witnesses—all with their different perspectives, agendas, talking points, fabrications, and sometimes out and out lies. But this was personal: and navigating through *his own* contradictory and inexplicable emotions regarding Mary Jones was not as easy as he hoped.

"Maybe we should go downstairs?" he finally said. It felt too—he searched in his brain for the perfect word—but all Leiv could come up with was *intimate.* He also didn't want to look around. Didn't want to *know* her place more than he already did, much less sit down.

As if reading his mind and sensing his inner turmoil, Mary laughed again, this time deeper and with what seemed to Leiv as more abandon. "Oh, don't be silly."

She walked over to what he guessed was a French settee and armchair arrangement. *Louis XVI maybe?* All he knew about European antiques was what Margaret and Mary herself had told him. The fabric was goldenish, and looked, he thought, rather faded. But then the light coming in Mary's west facing balcony French doors was thin, though he could make out crime scene tape running across the balcony. *Not just the street, but the balcony, too?* There were also multi-sectioned paned windows on the east wall of the large room, but the sun had moved higher into the sky, leaving Mary's parlor in a rather dreary dimness.

He knew crime scene protection and established forensics procedures did not dictate Glover should leave Mary alone in her apartment—and so near part of a crime scene. *Shame on you Glover*, he thought. But simultaneously admitted he probably would have done the same. *What is it about this woman?*

While Leiv took the few steps over to her settee as Mary had directed, and still not really wanting to look around, Mary said, "I know there's going to be questions about how Johnny ended up on the sidewalk outside my shop and underneath my balcony."

That's putting it mildly, he thought.

After he seated himself stiffly on what turned out to be a very uncomfortable settee, Mary finished what sounded to Leiv like a statement she prepared for his benefit. "If Glover can't do the question-asking that needs to be done, will you stay with me while the Deputy is here?" She sat down in a matching armchair.

Before he could answer, her smile faded almost immediately and she brought her right hand up to her forehead. "I keep feeling rather dizzy. Out of sorts." Mary slumped back into her armchair. "But I think it's mental. Seeing Johnny flying over my balcony, then lying on the sidewalk, not really knowing what happened."

"Can I get you some water or something? Tea? A drink?" Despite his reluctance, Leiv was forced to look around. There was a modest kitchenette area behind him, and a door he guessed led to a bedroom in front of him. All around were period pieces covered with keepsakes—or junk, depending on your perspective. *Just like her shop downstairs.*

"No, no." She waved him to remain seated, stiffened her

47

own back and sat up straighter. "I certainly don't want to be drunk when the Deputy Sheriff gets here." She managed a small smile again. "Besides, I have a new Hobnail Penny perfume bottle I want you to see. It's up here with me."

Leiv felt his eyes widen and his heart race at the mention of the perfume bottle. *Another one?*

"Not just like Naomi's, but special still." She looked at him for a long moment.

He was very glad he was not back in a courtroom, for Leiv feared Mary Jones would have completely flummoxed him—even back then—just as she was doing now.

"This one is amber in color. I think you'll like it." She smiled again, this time with a twinkle in her mesmerizing dark eyes. Eyes that had garnered her multitudinous fans in the world of soap operas.

Finally, he answered her earlier question. "Of course I'll stay," he said in the most confident voice his emotions allowed. *It's started,* he thought. Leiv couldn't quite put his finger on what. But *something* for sure. *Something* he most likely would run away from.

Wearing two hats was often difficult, but Charlie considered he was doing well on the "seasoned producer" maturity front. He had taken the time to pre-schmooze with Hermit Chan. *Now,* he and his crew were actually getting out of the filming van on the actual piece of property where PL's chimney stood. Chan's demurring on the chimney was even more incentive to check it out.

He was officially in filming mode. Even when heading for PL's chimney, they first stopped and filmed the alfalfa field along the road before arriving at what they concluded was the actual road to the land where the chimney stood. There was another alfalfa field further on down, closer to the town, but they turned back because this first field was in what PL dubbed "prime-flowering"—with bunches of little yellow butterflies making what ordinarily would be static-looking flowers, appear "alive" with movement.

In line with PL's desire to shoot at this particular field, Charlie's director's vision saw not only a status-quo picture of blue butterfly-enhanced flowers, but it would be great if those butterflies and alfalfa were in actual weather related movement—*if we could just get a slight breeze going.* He certainly did not want to come back with a petrol-powered wind-machine—even if he could find one within a couple hundred miles. Unfortunately, no breeze kicked in during their stop. *Maybe later today,* he thought at the time.

Now they were at the chimney location, and the sequence he wanted was a fade-in to a superimposed shot of the still standing house, with the burnt-out foundation and chimney of an earlier house as one piece of the total frame. Then for the scene's *pièce de résistance*—they would dissolve into a uncluttered and singular shot of the iconic chimney. All by itself, with a little 3D feel from angling the shot.

He was sure the chimney must be unique, even for the Mojave—*and with Marilyn's music.* Perfect. Charlie visualized himself in the cutting room, helping bring it all together for the Director's Cut. *My cut, my wrapping it up.*

He was smiling as they started up the path, his little movie-making troupe once again in single file behind him. Charlie's mind continued to whirr, and his insides jumped with joy; while at the same time, he hoped his "seasoned-producer" exterior reflected a calm and cool professionalism. Both parts of his personality nonetheless knew—the fireplace-prize awaiting them ahead was priceless.

Indeed, he heard PL exclaim with unabashed awe behind him, "Magnificent," as they came around the last bend and the chimney stood before them. He even heard Davey mutter behind him, "Not bad."

And an ancient school bus, Charlie noticed then immediately wondered if he could buy it from the owner. *Great prop for some film sometime.*

"I can't believe it," Pete said more to himself than to his team members. *If I'd paid more attention to my bearings during my flyover, I would have realized earlier the lay-of-the-land where we are right now.* Indeed, he didn't geographically note what a short drive it was from Hermit Chan's house to his stone chimney. Thinking back on this morning's fly-over, the first landmark he remembered from his helicopter adventure was the RV park close to I-40. Couldn't forget the big "DAD's" sign. Then came Chan's place, but he thought the castle as next. The chimney was actually next. Consequently, Pete was overjoyed.

The flowering alfalfa fields were quite something and a wonderful surprise. Now he was standing within view of the lonely-looking stone fireplace and iconic chimney which caught his eye and captured his photographic heart that very morning. Undeniably, the photographer in him was beyond pleased— *ecstatic,* he readily admitted to himself.

There was something special here, and he could feel excitement—kind of like an electric energy building within. Truthfully, he was still trying to wrap his mind around the "whole event" happening this morning. Nonetheless, Pete knew at that moment for sure—this shoot was going to be something special. *Beyond a photographic collaboration. Beyond awards.*

On the purely artistic level, Pete recognized this chimney was a symbol of a unique type of endurance. Though he wasn't sure yet on how to express his notion exactly—but guessed the underpinning of his concept was the human spirit, the desert, and pioneer days. *Somehow, I need to get that feeling of "early days" in this body of photography.* Pete even visualized their team huddled together in the cutting room, fussing over the Final Cut.

He felt his heart beat a little bit faster. And given this anticipatory state, Pete wanted to quicken his pace to catch up with Charley, David, and Marilyn who were forging ahead. Yet, he made himself slow down. Something within said he needed a still of this Chimney first.

Now. He needed to take a picture, now.

It would be his first up-close and personal sighting, so to speak, on this shoot. The alfalfa field was different—visual attractiveness. This was personal. Pete stopped—guessing he was maybe twenty-feet or so away, quieted himself, brought his SLR 35mm Canon up from his side, and prepared his settings. His prime lens, a 50mm 1:1.8 lens was attached. This was his snapshot camera—film, not digital—and "his baby." Perfect for what he wanted photographically to do right then.

When the chimney was framed as he wanted in his eye-level viewfinder—Pete's eye and lens captured a cracked, scrub-dessert-grass surrounded concrete foundation of about twenty-by-forty feet. The desert-grass broke through in many spots along haphazard crack lines in the foundation; while wind-blown pebbles and sand were strewn and collected in equally random patterns. A couple surviving pieces of weather-ragged wooden sill plates remained, giving a hint at the structure that once stood on the spot—but was now relegated to history. On the far eastern end of the foundation stood the brick fireplace. All rock, maybe twenty-feet tall—still precisely and snuggly fitted together.

When Pete snapped his picture, he knew his heart skipped a beat.

They were back standing in front of their window to the world; this time, Elizabeth-May had a mug of Constant Comment tea in her hand. The aroma was heavenly. But clearly, not "heavenly" enough to stop upcoming events.

Tempe's ears were up, his eyes intent and focused on the

outside, his stand rigid. He was on alert, and consequently Elizabeth-May followed his lead. She wasn't sure how Tempe knew invaders had arrived—but she'd seen the van coming down the road from the south just like the car a little bit earlier, and then when it hadn't reappeared heading on north, she figured something was up. Though, also like the white sedan, she couldn't be certain. But then when Tempe went on alert.

Too late to stop the intruders. One part of her wanted to just drop her mug, turn and run off with Tempe. Leave the world for just a wee-bit. Of course, she couldn't. Now they were here, invaders standing in the middle of her little universe—looking at her grandfather's great stone chimney as if it were one of the wonders of the world.

After Pete took his still picture, he followed the others to the edge of the chimney's burnt-out foundation. It was an interesting few moments for him. Not like actual "moments of silence," but none of their group said anything or moved for what he considered a remarkable number of frames—*at forty-eight frames per second*—his slow motion standard for movement. Even David, who Pete expected might have a smart-alecky comment ready, was standing silently and motionless in statue-like awe.

Not that the fireplace was particularly majestic, or grandiose, or towering. Consequently, Pete first speculated their seeming awe was a joint emotion of having arrived at "something." A place in their filming process. *A marker of sorts.*

"Should I go get Merlin?" Pete asked stepping in close to Charlie and breaking their silent and motionless tableau. "Merlin" was his newest Steadicam, and he had yet to use it with his Canon. His older and reliable stabilizer was a Flycam, but Charlie encouraged him to try different filming arrangements when the budget allowed—and Pete was itching to try Merlin on this film. Underlying his request about Merlin was Pete's eagerness to get started despite the reality he hardly needed a Steadicam to capture what he thought of as the chimney's essence.

"You're my expert on the right cameras," Charlie whispered out the side of his mouth. "But if you're asking, do I want this site in our documentary? Of course I do."

Charlie's words made Pete extremely glad he'd seen this monument of sorts from the helicopter this morning. It was a warm and pleasurable feeling. Emotional, even. And not just because Charlie liked the chimney, but more because up close and personal-like, all kinds of shots came to mind. He could visualize sweeping and pinpointed shots from the helicopter, and then here on the ground, a circular moving shot ending up with a close-up of the chimney. "I'm going to look around a bit before I drag our stuff up."

"I know, I know," Charlie said in a voice that told Pete he had his usual free rein.

Now standing on the "brink" of the foundation and of his film, Pete heard David say from his left, "And don't we need to talk to whoever lives in that house a little higher up?"

"Yes," Charlie quickly agreed. "I'll go see if anyone actually lives there." He sighed. "Might need releases and contracts. All the regular." He pulled out his cell phone and started to head up what looked to Pete like a seldom used walkway.

"Be careful," Pete said. "That path doesn't look like the most direct way to the house. I won't rush to start filming. I'll just look around a bit more first."

"Me, too," Marilyn said. "See over there?"

Pete turned slightly to look at an area on the other side of the foundation, almost directly across from the chimney. He nodded. What Pete saw were two weathered and slightly warped-looking doors, lying almost flat on the ground, with a rusted latch holding them together. "A bomb shelter?"

"A root cellar would be my guess." She smiled. "I need to get closer. Looks like a rotting stick in the latch, and…" her voice trailed off as she headed off.

Pete thought her smile pleasant. He also thought Marilyn LeBue was a darned good music director. Moreover, somewhere within, he knew he liked how she looked more than he should; especially after seeing her dressed like they all were, in jeans and chambray shirt variations. *Our filming uniforms.* But unlike the three men, she looked quite fetching—*while we just look scrubby*. Still, tight jeans and oversized shirt or not, fetching or not, Pete didn't believe in co-worker romances. *Maybe when this shoot is over.* Then almost immediately, he brought all his attention back to "the chimney." Marilyn and exploring a root cellar were quickly forgotten.

As Pete actually stepped from desert dust terrain onto the concrete remains of the house foundation, he made the step forward gingerly and with trepidation. He wasn't quite sure why. *It's not hallowed ground or anything like that.* Once he stepped over-the-line and onto the foundation of what had been someone's home in the past, whatever eeriness Pete felt vanished immediately and completely.

As he got closer, Pete become more impressed with the stature of the chimney, and amazed at what good shape it was in. "Whoever built this was quite a craftsman."

Surprisingly David had followed him rather closely, only about ten or so steps behind, and was in hearing range. "My grandfather was a stonemason way back when in Chicago I'm told. This chimney makes me wish I knew more about masonry."

"Yeah," Pete agreed, moving closer to the fireplace and chimney. "Like that curve over the fireplace-firebox. How the heck do they do that?"

"A *voussoir,* I think they're called."

Pete was fond of Davey, but gave him a look anyway.

"And keystone I believe is what that center one is called." David pointed toward the fireplace arch. "Holds the arch together."

Pete thought the size of the fireplace quite substantial and rather large for a homesteader-type American fireplace. He remembered an earlier documentary he worked on with Charlie called "American Abodes." His knowledge wasn't great on the fireplace topic, even after taking what seemed like *endless* stills of *endless* Early American fireplaces. "I bet I can almost stand in there," he said. Indeed, Pete had actually once stood in such a fireplace. But that was in England. Not in the United States.

"I doubt that." David's tone was clearly skeptical.

Once they were only feet away, it was quite clear his claim was hyperbole, but Pete liked the thought of being able to stand in a fireplace. When he'd stood in the one in England, it was cold despite the fact it was summer: and he almost shivered remembering. Then the thought of the English fireplace reminded him of the castle-like structure closer to Shiné he saw from the helicopter. *Don't want to miss that either.*

Oddly, as if his unconscious knew what was about to occur, and even though many pictures, images, and memories flooded through his mind and across his photographic eye, Pete set his camera gear down before stepping onto the still-in-place fireplace brick hearth. Then he next bent over, turned his head sideways and looked up into the chimney. When he used his hand to steady himself, Pete was almost immediately rewarded with a whoosh of soot-like material, followed by a square-ish object that hit him hard enough on the head to send him sprawling forward onto aged stones, surrounded by dirt and decaying matter—fortuitously missing smashing his head on cracked concrete or his nearby camera equipment.

Uncharacteristically, Pete cursed.

Ignoring Pete's condition, "It's some kind of book," David said, bending over to pick up the square-ish object. "Wrapped in plastic." Only then did he quickly add, "Are you okay?"

Actually, Pete felt like he'd been body-slammed, but before he had time to complain to Davey, behind him Marilyn screamed. He managed to prop himself up enough to look toward were he last saw her. She'd disappeared. And he knew where. Straight down into the bowels of what he guessed was a two-generation-old root cellar.

For a second time, Elizabeth-May almost dropped her much-adored diner-mug. Shakily, she set it down with both hands, bringing it to rest on a crocheted doily in the center of her round pedestal table—slightly to her and Tempe's rear. If she hadn't caught herself in time, her prized Route 66 embossed cup would have hit the wooden plank-floor below her feet rather hard, and most probably broken.

Her pedestal table boasted a rich-colored mahogany stain, and she kept it precisely placed, set back a bit out of harm's way from Tempe or herself, but centered on and in front of her picture-window in what she thought good light. She was also fond of the Victorian-styled cherub adorning her table's pedestal. With the table came the memory of her father bringing it home as a present for his mother. Unconsciously she took a step back, slightly closer to the table and memories, and maybe out of sight from prying eyes looking in. *I can't run now.*

She could still see out quite well, and with Tempe at her side, Elizabeth-May watched the man leading the invaders as he started up her front pathway for a second time. He turned back when that silly woman fell into her Grandma Elizabeth's root cellar. He looked to be excited and talking into his cell phone as he approach her house.

My sanctuary no more. Secrets no more.

"Hard to get a signal out here," she told Tempe—then laughed, short and ironically at her inane thought at such a dire time. Then she forced her hands to her side, but unconsciously still tightened her fists until she felt her fingernails biting into her hands. She forced them to relax. *Calling the police. That's what he's doing.*

When the news a filming crew was coming to Shiné first started circulating, a little voice had tried to break through, warn her, ringing alarm bells. *But no,* she'd blithely ignored the premonitions and stomach harbingers. Forced them away and pushed her fear of discovery back into its hidey-hole.

Lost in apprehensive thought, a long moment passed before Elizabeth-May realized she was barely breathing. She took a deep breath and forced one hand from her side and touched the glass. It had turned from warm to icy cold.

Oh Hermit, how could you? Tempe moaned softly as if he were reading her thoughts.

Then it clicked. Hermit didn't betray her—gotten caught up in the filming. *No,* the invaders saw it from that darned helicopter going over this morning.

Damn flying machines.

"I wanted you to know." Mary Jones's voice was soft but strong, and it was as if her words were spoken into a world just for him alone.

Leiv was looking out the French doors that opened to a balcony which he was sure gave a view of Main Street below. Crime scene tape continued to block him from actually going out onto the balcony, and he wondered if Glover was standing in the same spot below where he left him. What Leiv could see from Mary Jones' second floor French door windows were the tops of the few one-story storefronts across the street. One of which, several rooftops to the right and north, was Shiné's Police Station. A huge unit of some kind sat atop Glover's office, but Leiv could only guess at its purpose. *A cooling unit?*

Suddenly, he felt like he was in the middle of a not-so-funny comedy-skit on a late night TV show. The dead body of disgraced soap opera star lying on the concrete sidewalk below, waiting for an out-of-town medical examiner, covered with a tartan drop cloth, guarded by a singular and rigid-standing Gary Cooper-styled Chief of Police. No gawkers, no news people—nothing to mark this as the special happening it actually was.

On top of that, he was standing in an antique-saturated apartment above the scene, going through some kind of emotional turmoil with the prime suspect for the homicide. A prime suspect who had time and opportunity to do whatever she wanted with any potential evidence. A comedic skit turned into a soap opera. *Or a thirties era murder mystery?*

Only in Shiné. Leiv wondered what LC would think about all this, and another quote from LC's journal came to him out of nowhere. *"And sometimes, just touching something, any old thing...and you can end up knowing what's going to happen. Sometimes, even what's already happened. Kinda like you're inside their head."*

How could LC know about Mary Jones, and how could Leiv ignore what had happened just moments earlier, when Mary Jones—for the second time in their knowing each other—asked him to touch one of her collectables? Another Hobnail Penny perfume bottle. No matter it was amber instead of blue, no matter it was smooth rather than crater-pocked like the last one. It was an identical experience. Unsettling, unwanted, and most disturbing.

Now she sat watching him, rather calmly he thought, given what had just passed between them.

Only minutes earlier, in the muted dimness of Mary's sitting room, him uncomfortably perched in the corner of her settee, scooted almost to the front edge and facing her—she'd stretched her arm and hand out toward him, the perfume bottle seemingly defying gravity by sitting perfectly still and balanced on the imperfect surface of the palm of her hand.

He'd reached out and touched it. And they'd communicated.

Now, looking out as he was over the rooftops, with

Mojave scrub desert in the distance, and Lookout Loop and Shiné Ridge in the far distance, Leiv sighed. *I need to tell her what I felt.*

Mary interrupted his thought and resolve. "I guess I should tell you, my producer and the studio in LA are having some lawyer call me. Said to keep my mouth shut until he does." She laughed. "Margaret Deers was coming in to sit with me. I called her and said stay home, Dear."

Leiv wasn't sure what kind of laugh Mary's was. Derisive, amused, happy? Then again, before he could mention the perfume bottle, or further decipher her laugh, a loud phone somewhere behind her rang.

"You have a landline?" Leiv said, asking about the obvious. So did he. *Luddites, the both of us.*

She stood to go answer it. "Can't stand those little cell phone things. I'm guessing that's the lawyer."

Immediately he remembered the huge 1892 Rotary Eiffel Tower replica monstrosity she had down in her shop, and wondered what kind of antique reproduction she was answering here in her apartment behind him. Then, as if mocking his perceived technology attitude, his cell phone in his jeans jacket rang, startling Leiv enough to jump slightly.

When he saw the caller's name, Leiv answered immediately and heard Glover say, "Brad Temper and a team just arrived to take over here, and he'll be up there where you are any minute to talk to her. And Pastor Apply's going out to Lizzy's as soon as he can. I need him to hold her hand. And you need to get down here right now if you want to ride with me." After a slight pause, and sounding almost like an afterthought, he added, "We've got another body. Out at Elizabeth-May Logan's place."

Mary Jones's telephone conversation was a quick one. Confirmation, yes, a lawyer would be in town soon. Coming by airplane from LA. *Probably newspaper vans would be next, then the paparazzi.* She wanted to cry, and was disgusted she wanted to.

She then looked to Leiv, intently trying to assess his emotions without letting him know she was. He was still holding his cell phone—though his call also seemed completed. He seemed to be staring unfocused into her parlor, and she could tell from his expression he was surprised. She consequently intuited another extraordinary event had happened. *As if your ex-husband appearing out of the blue in the middle of the night wasn't enough.* Then dizziness and a sense of wobbliness, even though she was sitting, again came out of nowhere. *Just like on the balcony.*

Something else was definitely going on with Leiv. *Connected to me?* She couldn't be sure, and definitely wasn't receiving any conclusive signals. Nothing like what she shared with Leiv through the little bottles. *What a surprising connection that turned out to be. Quite remarkable.*

Then another touch of lingering vertigo caused Mary to bring her hand to her head. *It's just so much to take in.* Max appearing out of nowhere. What was going to happen next? And Max's troubling claim some guy named Alex was coming after him for monies owed. *Gambling debts.* The gambling part wasn't a surprise, but a "hit" man as he put it—coming after him? *Unbelievable.*

"I'm going to have to leave you," Leiv said. He looked her way and asked. "Are you okay? Has your dizziness come back?"

"No, no. You go, I'll be fine," she urged him. "Besides I believe Glover said a doctor would be coming from Needles along with the deputy. I'm not sure where Doc Walker is right now." She thought Leiv still looked in genuine distress whether to go or stay. "Go," she added firmly. "Glover needs you."

Following close after he left, Mary heard heavy footsteps coming up her stairs. She took a deep breath and tried to prepare herself for the Needles detective. *Where the heck was Will?* She needed to talk to him about last night.

She thought she heard his voice, this morning, outside—

but wasn't sure. "He needs to contact me," she said to her momentarily empty apartment. She rubbed her forehead a third time. *Oh dear,* she thought to herself.

Deputized Walker Johns was at his side, pen and notebook in hand, as Glover asked, "And you are?" Simultaneously Glover offered his hand to Charlie White.

With an eager-looking expression, Charlie firmly exchanged his handshake, gave his name, a brief description of how and why they arrived where they were, then introduced his film team, one by one. The sun was getting higher and hotter and Glover could feel his own temperature responding. The producer's hand, out of sync with the increasing temperature, was cool and dry.

As stand-in deputy, Walker also had a voice recorder attached to his belt. Glover disingenuously explained to Walker earlier their blanket disclaimer, "Hope you don't mind, we take this all down," covered written and audio.

Right before calling Leiv to come out to Elizabeth-May's, Glover had already chosen—partly because of necessity, but also from experience—to close his office in Shiné and have Walker Johns follow him out to the Logan place to help with documenting what happened. His instincts said he didn't want to assess the accuracy of witness statements, secure the scene, make decisions about calling in help from other parts of San Bernardino County—*and* take notes at the same time.

Then, when first arriving at Elizabeth-May's, before entering the action himself, Glover made a quick assessment of the scene from his cruiser; besides issuing several code 10s and initial incident reports to both the County and State, Glover also put in a call directly to the SBC Coroner's Forensics team himself. Walker was technically Shiné's part-time Ambulance Technician, certified as such, and had some experience with crime, witness emotionality, and dead bodies, but he wasn't a forensics expert. He needed the best this morning.

Those same instincts had told Glover to get Leiv on the scene to do what he was hoping to do himself—watch, listen, take in the scene. *He sees things I don't. And he won't have everyone staring at him while I will.* Recognizing and admitting Leiv's uncanny competence at this point in their acquaintance was easy. After several years being around the man, he'd come to like him, and respected his keen mind. His mother Margaret thought the same, which was an additional high recommendation in his mind. *Of course she would, Leiv and I having the same father.*

Glover's initial assessment of this very much "looking-like-LA" film group, was they all appeared a little shaken. As an aside, he did wonder about what Charlie White's requirements for Milhouse might be. *Who the hell needs a set-designer in the middle of the Mojave? Dirt is dirt, for goodness' sake.*

Having just been pulled out of a dirty hole occupied by a dead body, Marilyn LeBue, the Music Director, remained quite visibly shaken. She was still coughing intermittently, and swiping at her hair and face as if those simple actions would banish the spider webs, dust, and plant detritus stuck to her body and clothes—maybe even make disappear the memory of what she'd fallen in on.

And the photographer Pete Lily didn't look that much better in the dirt department. Glover almost smiled at the thought of the tall and lanky-looking man sticking his head up that chimney.

Glover wanted to wait for forensics—but in this case, he thought it was quite unreasonable to expect Marilyn not to clean up. Having Walker bag all her clothes would have to suffice. Hopefully she had a change of clothes in their van. *Maybe a lock of her hair if she was willing.* For sure, she needed to go shower and calm herself somewhere—and soon; seeing a real dead body wasn't the same as an actor laying on the floor on a stage-set. He didn't think he needed anything from David Milhouse—*except for the book.*

Not in line with standard crime scene assessment guideline questions, Glover asked, "Are you the Charlie White who's making the film 'Route 66—Then and Now'?"

"You know about the film?" Glover thought Charlie's face reflected child-like pleasure and surprise.

Glover clicked out the side of his mouth. "We take a lot of pride in Route 66 in these parts." Glover thought his own words as he heard them leave his mouth could have come straight from a 1950's Western.

Seemingly reading his mind by the look on his face, Charlie's words came out in tune with Glover's words. "High Noon is one of my favorite movies. Much more complicated movie than a first viewing would indicate."

Glover had to clear his throat, swipe at his nose with the back of his hand, then look at the ground for a few seconds to fill the moment necessary for him to maintain his professional demeanor. Charlie White's words could have come straight out of his own mouth. *How could he possibly know I was thinking about Westerns? And that one in particular?*

Also in the span of that moment, he sensed with this move-maker, though very different from him in many ways, there was some like-minded connection he couldn't quite put his finger on. He liked him. Similar to Leiv, in that they had quite different personalities, but over the last few months, he'd come to appreciate in how many ways they did fit. *Funny that.* With Leiv, he figured part of the "simpatico" feeling was due to the judge-thing—a law and order kind of connection. But Charlie White was in the movie biz. *How could they be connected?*

As Charlie walked away from Glover, the front end of Pastor Apply's noisy dark-blue Volvo station wagon appeared coming up the approach road to Elizabeth-May's. In watching Apply, he noticed Elizabeth-May still had that school bus sitting on her property. He'd tried to buy it off her several times, but she refused.

Slow to get here, Glover thought, returning his focus to Apply. *Morning Bible School*, he realized on second thought. Apply should know why he asked for him to come out, and hopefully he'd just pass them by and head straight to the house and Elizabeth-May. She was one of the pastor's parishioners, and like Mary, he thought she might need some emotional support.

Glover next heard the approaching wail of an ambulance in the distance. He was amazed—*too soon* it seemed—but he was grateful nevertheless, and wondered if SBC's forensics team was right behind them. No one else on scene seemed to notice the high frequency whine except Walker.

"CHP probably called an ambulance in from Baker," Walker offered.

Of course. Which meant however, SBC Forensics would still be a long time in coming. Internally he bemoaned, another crime-scene he had to secure for a length of time, and what were his remaining resources here at Elizabeth-May's? A deputized Ambulance Technician, Leiv Rhodes, and his assigned counselor for Elizabeth-May, Pastor Apply? He guessed about now SBC Brad Temper would also be needing some more help in Shiné at Le Bric-à-Brac. Two crime scenes competing for the same resources. Glover almost cursed, but caught himself in time.

Instead, he turned away from Charlie White, who oddly Glover thought, was watching him even though ostensibly talking to Leiv—*producer actions no doubt. Seeing this as a movie?* The thought didn't anger him, and he wasn't sure why not. He knew this was real life, not a movie.

Glover walked away a few steps, turned his back on the entire scene, then called Brad on his cell phone to ask him if he had a friend in CHP who could get both of them some police or forensics help pretty darned quick. *Or*, did his boss maybe *know* someone who could. "We need help."

Even though he was turned away, and even though he had just critiqued Charlie White's action, Glover noticed his own "eyes in the back of his head" were simultaneously keeping tabs on Leiv and Charlie White—both now standing and talking right in front of the burnt out fireplace. His peripheral vision was quite good—and evidently so was his personal rear-view mirror. Leiv picked up a rock from the ground and slipped it into his pocket.

Mugs was PO'd. Mainly because he might only have himself to blame for his current predicament. He ran his finger around his sport-shirt collar, and found his skin was damp. *Damn desert heat.* And he felt like he needed to sneeze. *Damn desert dust.*

He'd waited too long. Should have gone right in, shaken the location of Anthony L's ledger out of that feeble old broad, *wouldn't be hard*, then bashed her over the head for helping her husband hide out in the first place. *Come on, Mugs, that's screwy thinking. It isn't her fault you waited, now is it?* And screwy thinking was something he prided himself on never doing. Too many had gotten into hot water that way.

No, the fact was, he was stuck out in the middle of a god-forsaken desert, sitting on an aching butt and not able to escape because of Anthony L. *Ah.* That was better, his anger subsided a little; having someone else to blame was a tonic-bottle Mugs often found comfort and mental relief in taking a swig from.

Unfortunately, he was also getting hotter. *And it's only spring.* He wanted to curse aloud, but dare not make a sound.

At least he thought to throw a bottle of water in his fixer-bag: and he was well hidden, sitting on his haunches almost in the middle of the Athols now, his car only see-able if you came up the near invisible little track he'd found. *I'm good at that kind of thing. Hiding out. Lying low.* Still his butt hurt. Desert dirt was not the same as padded auto seats.

He rubbed his mouth and chin with the long slender fingers. Admittedly, that film crew van had surprised him—then that maneuver with the chimney and the book falling out. Pulled out, or accident? He wasn't sure.

That body in that hole though. Unconsciously he shook his head and licked his lips. They tasted salty—but also a little sweet. Who would have thought some old codger's body would show up just when he needed to do a "fix." All he wanted to do was snatch Anthony L's ledger, then move on. *Well, at least I know where the damn book is now.*

Maybe down the road, the whole thing might make a good story, but right now, a damn bunch of movie-making-posers snatching his book and finding a body was not part of his plan. Or funny. For a moment, Mugs did wonder about the body that stupid woman was screaming about, yelling for them to get her out. But now, he didn't give a damn. He needed to…well, he needed to do something. Mugs puffed out both sides of his mouth, sending out two heavy streams of air—but noiselessly, like his curses. *I'd sure want out of that hole, too.* The woman looked terrified when they pulled her out. Of course he'd seen a few dead bodies in his time. Falling in a hole on top of one, though, that would be a different can of worms.

Going back to pondering his own circumstances again, Mugs rubbed his forehead this time, felt real sweat, and recognized with renewed clarity the consequences of his decision to hang around.

Now a stupid station wagon is coming up the drive. "Son of a—" Mugs started to say aloud, but caught himself in time. *Been here too long to blow my cover now.* Fortunately, his rental was well hidden, but the first chance he saw, Mugs knew he needed to get the "heck out of Dodge City." Then it hit him. He jumped up and grabbed his bag. *No more waiting, now's the time to make his escape.* Who's going to notice a nice new quiet rental-motor while that old wagon is lumbering up the drive? Once again, his instincts as the best "fixer" around came into play. *Wily like a coyote, I am.* It was a phrase Mugs' Uncle Harry used. And often spouted simultaneous with his other hackneyed saying, "Now is the time."

Mugs also noticed most precisely—Anthony L's ledger

was handed over to that cop and his sidekicks.

I'll have to change that.

Was that an ambulance he heard in the distance? He shook his head. *This desert is doing a number on me.*

Leiv also took notice of Pastor Apply's wagon coming up the drive. Though for a few seconds or so, he thought he might have heard a second motor, which didn't make sense, given everyone else at the scene was parked. He quickly dismissed what he heard, or thought he heard, as an echo. Sounds in the desert had played tricks on him before—like traveling farther than expected, or producing directional confusion.

He was glad for Apply's pastoral appearance. He'd just palmed a rock he didn't know what to do with, and someone needed to be in there talking to Elizabeth-May. He likewise thought of Mary, probably still feeling alone, though Brad Temper was for sure still on the scene. *And dealing with an interrogation by a Sheriff's deputy must be scaring her to death.* Okay, she was an actress, a soap opera actress no less, and had dealt with worse situations in her scripts. *On the set. On screen.*

Leiv was aware his rambling thoughts were because he was still reeling from his visit with Mary Jones earlier, and his encounter with her latest Hobnail Penny perfume bottle. But before his mind, emotions, and maybe even his heart could take all "that" in, here he was, faced with another body. *And a mysterious book, no less.*

A book he was dying to look at. *A book* Walker had quickly taken possession of from Charlie White. A perfume bottle, a body on the sidewalk on Main Street, a book in a chimney at Elizabeth-May's, and a body in a long defunct root cellar. *Worthy of a Perry Mason episode.* He almost smiled at his step back in time to his youthful pre-lawyer days. Even now, among the seemingly endless reruns, Leiv occasionally watched one on TV, and was abashed he still retained the occupational fantasy of being the judge presiding over one of his idol's cases.

He and Glover had shared little during the ride south out of town to Elizabeth-May's. *Maybe he's a little stunned, too?* Though he doubted it. Not for the first time, Leiv recognized that in his mind—Glover needed to live up to a larger-than-life image. His friend, though quite smart, was also the "tough guy," balancing against his "arbitrator" from the bench and mild-mannered "thinking man" persona. *Yes*, it was becoming evident to Leiv, significant and dramatic events were happening right now—involving both of them, and drawing on both of their skills.

Consequently, mentally returning to and visually taking in the scene in front of him, Leiv willed his mind clear—pushing his relationships with Mary Jones and Glover back into their storage compartments. Glover and Walker were expecting him to be looking around. Taking in. The Chief had brought him along for a reason—he was shorthanded for sure—but he hoped Glover actually wanted him at his side. Looking. Listening. Thinking. Leiv also figured he had set himself up last winter, "figuring" stuff out. *Funny that. Just blind luck.* And now he was stuck with the results of his prior success.

Although, in several retrospective moments, Leiv had admitted to himself and his grandfather—he rather enjoyed trying to solve the puzzles. Far more complicated and mentally stimulating than following "precedents and procedures" to make rulings from the bench; a logical, morally upright, and important endeavor he still thought. But seldom creative. *Though a couple times I did do some finagling.* He certainly didn't disparage his years on the bench. *Wonderful years.* This was different, though. And enjoyable.

Another frank assessment Leiv found himself facing up to over the last few months was that helping Glover, was also helping him move forward a bit. In particular—move past his grief and lingering guilt still haunting him after Melissa's death in Chicago.

Even now, under a pale-blue picture-perfect Shiné late morning sky, the air warming rapidly, a scruffy but eager-looking film crew waiting to be scrutinized, a dead body probably still lying on the pavement back in Shiné, and now an additional dead body in a root-cellar awaiting his attention and critical eye—that horrible night in Chicago forced its way forward. For a long moment, Leiv was helpless to stop the memories with their accompanying still-vivid pictures. And even though standing where he was, just feet away from Glover, Walker, and the others—he wanted to turn and run back to the safety of Rhodes Castle. As if physically fleeing the scene would stop his reliving those moments in Chicago. Revisiting his pain.

...Hearing Melissa—her sweet words. "What a lovely evening." Her voice lilting and harmonic—a little bit of song always there.

Chicago. Hundreds of thousands of cars drove on I-290 as it miraculously, it seemed, went under the Chicago Post Office. Yes, they were on the "Ike" that night, or the Congress Expressway, depending on your generation. He and Melissa knew it as the quickest way to head west and get out of the city.

It was Fall, had rained all day, and an overcast night was engulfing the city. Leiv was tired, and figured Melissa was too. Hence the driver.

Even with Elizabeth-May's iconic chimney marking the real moment in time he needed to deal with—his memories refused to recede.

...the back of their limousine driver's head was vividly still in his memory. The front interior light must have been on. Why? A question he still didn't know the answer to.

Then waking up in the hospital, after a week in a coma, he was told. No memories until Melissa's sobbing sister at the side of his hospital bed told him she was dead. Then she'd slapped him, cursed him forever for meeting her sister. I should have been driving. Not called for a car.

"Are you the man with the Castle?" Pete was asking him, standing directly in front of Leiv and forcing his thoughts back into the present and the task at hand. "I'd offer you my hand, but it's dirty with soot and God only knows what. Cleaned them off several times now."

"Yes." Leiv hoped he didn't sound as relieved as he felt to be jerked back into the present by Pete Lily. "We call it Rhodes Castle. And you're the photographer? Right?"

Pete laughed, and Leiv liked the tone of his amusement.

"Is it the fact I'm lugging this camera crap around a dead give away?" Pete held his Canon up with both of his soot-stained hands in a gesture indicating he was teasing. "I'm afraid I'm pretty darned dirty." He glanced back and gestured toward the chimney. "Could have been worse I guess. Could have hurt my camera."

"I'd say." Leiv laughed at Pete's use of the word "hurt" versus "damaged" when talking about his camera. Memories of Melissa were fast moving back into their hidey-hole. "That camera actually looks pretty heavy. And expensive. It's hard to get that soot off your hands sometimes—hope your camera isn't damaged. Have a fireplace myself."

Pete blew out a stream of air. "Yeah, just lucky I'd set my camera down on the foundation before sticking my head in that chimney." He shook his head. "On the camera weight, you get used to it. It's all the extras making the bag look so gargantuan." Pete then started moving away, heading toward their van it looked like. "Wait until you see the monstrosity I'll be lugging back..." he paused for a few seconds. "...though, I'm not sure if I need the Steadicam." Then he stopped, seemingly deep in camera selection considerations.

But Leiv had an idea, and when he looked over at Glover he realized from the slight nod the Chief sent his way even though talking to Marilyn LeBue—he must have been watching him and Pete—and Leiv fancied they were both on the same wave length. Consequently, he interrupted Pete's perceived decision-making. "So, you're planning on taking pictures of..." he looked around with added hand gestures, "all this for your movie?"

"Yeah." The look on Pete's face said, *how could I not?*

"You've probably noticed, our Police Chief is short-handed here, and there will be a wait before a forensics team arrives."

Pete's face lit up, and the eagerness in his voice was unavoidable. "And you want me to document the scene like they do in TV crime shows?" He sounded like a kid.

"If that's not too much—" Before Leiv could finish his request Pete had placed his bag on the ground, had camera in his hand, and was panning the area, including getting a shot of him before he moved forward. Pete was on the job within seconds.

Another glance Glover's way and he saw Shiné's Chief of Police was smiling. Once again Leiv's fancy leapt to also seeing him wink. All the while knowing Glover was too far away to see such an action, even if he *had* actually winked. What he did know was he needed to look around himself. Do what Pete was now doing, but with his own senses. Do what Glover expected him to do.

Leiv started by turning his attention to Elizabeth-May's current house about six hundred or so feet up the drive from where they stood in the remainder of her first home. Pastor Apply's Volvo was now parked squarely in front of her wooden entry steps. Starting with those wide steps and veranda, Elizabeth-May's rebuilt home was similar to Rhodes Castle by Leiv's way of thinking, in that it conjured up an older period, a different time, and was built in a style *not* evocative of the Mojave Desert. Though if pressed, Leiv knew he couldn't yet come up with an archetypical "Mojave" architectural style their houses actually clashed with. The shorthand version was—though quite different from each other, neither house "fit."

Besides the porch steps and veranda, her current house was two-story, on a foundation raised almost to an English basement height, a bay window on the first and second floor, with a modest copula and accompanying widow's walk atop.

With a regretful-sounding sigh prompted by thoughts of days long gone, Leiv slowly turned himself around in a full circle, taking in what both forensic experts, and filmmakers he thought, would call "the scene." And despite the two-story nature of Elizabeth-May's current house, and also given it was on a slight hillock, what insisted on catching his eye and holding Leiv's interest was the scorched chimney and fireplace from the Logan's first house. Again, a remnant of days long gone pulled at his sensibilities the most.

"Amazing," he said aloud.

"I bet you're talking about the chimney," Charlie White said, coming over to stand next to him.

"Indeed," Leiv answered affably, hoping not to let on the man surprised him enough to nearly make him jump. "You're the movie-maker, right?" Leiv offered his hand and name. "And clearly a mind reader."

After they shook hands, Charlie explained, "Not really a mind reader. Just a lot a time spent watching PL do the same sweeping appraisal you just did."

"PL?"

"Pete Lily. Our photographer. You were just talking to him."

Charlie White was clearly observant. *A watcher.* "I guess to be an award-winning producer you have to be an observant type of person."

"Well...." Charlie's face displayed curiosity and maybe a touch of alarm.

"Not to worry about me knowing why you're here in Shiné." Leiv smiled. "Chief Deers is a fan of Route Sixty-six everything. He clued me in when he told me you were coming to

Shiné."

Charlie laughed fully while simultaneously looking over toward Glover, who was now talking to Pete. The producer's demeanor and facial expression turned somber almost immediately. "Hope I wasn't too loud. I guess this could be considered a crime scene?" Nonetheless, abashed or not, he seemingly couldn't hold back his amusement indefinitely. "I'm really sorry, Mr. Rhodes. But if you could see the look on your face. Priceless." He brought his hand to his mouth, clearly trying not to laugh loudly again. "The look of amazement—incredulity actually that's still there—at the idea that someone would want to document this part of the Mojave. Route Sixty-six or not."

Leiv had to laugh himself—though softly and befitting the scene, he hoped. He liked this man who could use the word "incredulity" in everyday conversation and not seem snooty. When he was able to speak with a straight face, Leiv said, "I must have given Chief Deers the same look when he first told me about your coming here. From him, however, I got an earful. A lengthy instructional tongue-lashing about the history everywhere you look around here."

Charlie nodded and looked over at Glover again. "You must be friends."

"We are." Before he could say more, David called out, "Need some help, here." He was precariously holding Marilyn LeBue up by one arm. It looked to Leiv like she fainted, or was about to.

Glover was quickly at Marilyn's other side to help support her, and just as quickly was one-handedly patting his uniform pants pocket. Leiv and Charlie quickly followed Glover's lead and rushed to where they were standing, while Pete and Walker were evidently too involved in a forensics-documentation effort, and didn't immediately rush over.

Leiv figured Glover wanted to try getting more medical help on his cell. "Do you have a home base yet?" Leiv asked in general while taking over Glover's supporting position next to

Marilyn so he could more easily make the call.

David spoke up before anyone else could. "I'm in charge of logistics and arranging things like that. I kind of screwed-up there. So now I'm thinking we go south back to I-Forty and over to Ludlow, or go all the way north up to I-Fifteen and find something in Baker."

A quick and passing nausea overtook Leiv for a moment. Ignoring the feeling, he shot a quick "desert" conspiratorial glance at Charlie, who in his turn, wasn't able to keep from smiling back at him. "You evidently thought there would be a motel in Shiné?" Leiv asked with the same incredulity Charlie had just chided him over.

"Yeah, I did."

Marilyn seemed to be catching her breath. Up close as he was, Leiv could see she was covered in dirt and dust from the top of her head to her designer hiking boots—and the odor from the "mess" she'd fallen into was one he'd never smelled before. *That's why my nausea.* In his past life, samples of various items in all shapes and forms had been brought into his court as evidence—many stomach-churning, but never any substance he was required to smell. *Thank goodness.* Of course he'd been told "stories" by cops. He hadn't really appreciated the odor-factor in their stories until this moment.

Out the corner of his eye, Leiv caught a glimpse of Glover, now a few steps away talking on his cell phone and thought his friend was looking their way and about to say something to him and Charlie. But before the Chief of Police could interject his opinion or instructions, Leiv said, "When the Chief is through here, follow me back to my place. I think Ms. LeBue could do with a shower the moment she's free to go."

Marilyn shifted her weight and bestowed a grateful smile his way. Leiv smiled at her in return and was glad he invited them all to Rhodes Castle before Glover could object.

But before David had time to formally accept or reject his offer—Glover appeared out of what Leiv thought was thin air given where he was standing seconds earlier—and to Leiv's relief and surprise, agreed in a no-nonsense tone which wasn't quite a command, but decidedly more than a polite pleasantry. "Excellent idea," Glover said.

Glover then turned to Pete and Walker who had finally joined them. "Since you've been so obliging and helpful so far, could you get all the shots Deputy Johns thinks we need for forensics Mr. Lily?" His tone was commanding, while also considerate and caring. To the music director, he said, "Of course we need all your clothes bagged, Ms. Lebue after you've showered at Mr. Rhodes's place." Then a mischievous smile appeared and Glover looked to Leiv directly. "Maybe HM could rustle up some sandwiches or something for lunch?"

Rustle up? He knew Glover loved westerns, but now he was starting to talk like he was in the old west. Leiv almost smiled, but didn't want to give him the pleasure. *Still,* he thought, Glover was an amazing man, and once again living up to the image he expected of him.

"Is that an ambulance I hear?" Charlie asked.

"Doubt it so soon," Glover said.

Leiv knew he was lying because he could hear it. *Glover probably knew about the ambulance already.* But before he could admire or criticize Glover for whatever trickery he was navigating, the ambulance wail got louder, and for an emotional moment he couldn't hold back—Leiv even while still steadying Marilyn, was again in Chicago on highway pavement cradling Melissa's head, with whipping red and white ambulance lights cutting through the darkest, coldest, and cruelest night of his life. He managed to push the horrible memories away. Barely.

Hester couldn't remember ever crying in her life; but several times this morning, she'd come close. Consequently when Leiv called about having guests—*he'll never know because I'll never tell him*—the ground under her feet was shaking a bit. After hanging up though, she was composed enough to say, "Well, at least he said 'please.'" Her tone was half-complaining, half-complimenting, as if her audience, Dobie, lying underneath the kitchen table, could understand her nuanced delivery.

For once, the Doberman wasn't stretched out as was her habit across the kitchen doorway threshold. And she wasn't asleep, but seemingly paying attention to Hester's cooking efforts and listening to her occasional comments.

In truth, his call somehow had taken a bit of the edge off her funk, and Hester was honest enough with herself these days to know it would be hard for Leigh-Everett to do much of *anything* she actually approved of. So, she let his words and attitude appease her some—right now at least. However, she also knew she would persist in her biased ill will, calling him some form of idiot whenever she could, and whenever the opportunity appeared down the road. *One of life's little pleasures.*

Though this time, it really was hard to be too upset with Everett's no-count son. From early this morning when she eavesdropped when that busybody Margaret's son Glover called, Hester had been dying to know what was going on. *Now*, Leigh-Everett had invited a film crew to come over, stay in The Castle even. This was quite a development, and she wanted to know every bit about what was going on. Somehow, she needed to get all the details. Consequently, she wasn't as PO'd as she could let herself get, and even felt rather excited about making lunch and getting rooms ready for visitors. Not a big deal really. Like her mother, Hester Miller Senior, she kept a tiptop house. Visitors expected or not.

She even felt a spurt of enthusiasm. For a few months now, Hester had retreated more and more into her kitchen with her friend Dobie. One of her great comforts was, she thought the dog also realized Leigh-Everett was not the man his father or grandfather were. And consequently, Dobie had chosen her over Leigh-Everett. Wishful thinking maybe? *As if the dog could possibly know....*

While pulling hamburger out of the freezer for her "Romani Stew," then potatoes, celery, and onions—always a hit—Hester let her flip-flop thoughts about Leigh-Everett backslide. "Being a big-time judge doesn't make you a 'man,'" she clarified for Dobie's benefit.

It was so exciting conspiring with Nadya Collins to steal the Mojave-Stone from right under the idiot's nose and return it to Cooper hands. Together, they would prove he wasn't up to his father or grandfather. *I was so tricky. Yep, from right under his nose.*

Then, partly to help her not think about subsequent non-events with Nadya and what might have gone wrong—and partly because she actually liked cooking, especially for occasions like today—Hester decided to also make another batch of yeast bread. This one huge.

She also wanted to take her mind off her frustration with her equally dimwitted family in Chicago. She tended toward making huge batches of bread, too much trouble not to. This time she would additionally make little rolls. Perfect for a party, and the yeast aroma would go all over the castle. Then she could have loaves for in the morning, or maybe sliced for toast?

"I'll shape them into little mini-loaves, then freeze them." She was now talking to a sleepy looking Dobie who had repositioned herself, and stretched out in front of her state-of-the art double oven.

Looking over at Dobie, Hester admitted, "Guess I do have to give Leigh-Everett credit for doing a good job on the upgrades." Her kitchen would be hard to match, even in any "home-beautiful" magazines. Hester certainly wished she could blame her Mojave-stone misery on Leigh-Everett. But she couldn't. *It's those damn Coopers letting me down.* Her Lovel cousins in particular.

Here I am. Waiting. Months passed, and still no letter from Nadya confirming the Mojave-Stone was now safely in Cooper hands. *Nothing.* And the really painful part, the worst part—

Nadya had almost felt like a daughter; well a niece at least. And still no calls, no letters.

She did hear Sydney applied for a divorce from Nadya through Leigh-Everett, but nothing directly from Nadya on that front either. *And after all the sneaking around we did.*

Hester allowed herself a little smile amidst her now building anger, reliving that night again in her revelry as she started some fresh yeast proofing, found her starter in the back of the refrigerator, and rummaged for her special miniature-loaf baking pans. Her starter used potato flakes as a key ingredient, and had been kept continuously alive for at least two generations that she knew about in one refrigerator or other.

She even sent several letters to the address Nadya left—each a little more urgent than the last. Nothing in reply.

The phone rang again, and now successfully back into a foul mood, Hester sighed heavily. Indeed, she couldn't remember feeling so low in months. She wasn't much of an out loud curser, but she did think, *damn cousins, damn Mojave-Stone.*

"Rhodes residence," she answered the now annoying phone in her snootiest tone. Then immediately regretted it. It was Leiv again, confirming how many guests they were going to have. Quickly she tried to rein in her emotions. Something was going on in town, she could tell from the Police Chief's voice when she'd listened in earlier, and she wanted to now know what it was. Leigh-Everett probably wasn't going to tell her outright, *although his tone has seemed friendlier lately.* She further uncharitably surmised after he hung up, *he wants something. Wants to tell me something.* Something bigger than guests. "Guess I'll find out soon enough."

Glover Deer's voice she liked, even though she thought something must be wrong with him from the start, wanting to stay here in the desert. Of course his mother lived in Shiné—and on further thought, Hester begrudgingly admitted that was probably a good enough reason to stay. Hadn't she stayed because there had always been a Miller woman in the house since

LC built the place and Viola hired the first staff? *I stayed because of my mother, too.*

She could see Dobie was sleeping for real now, but she continued to confide in her anyway. "Maybe I should go back to Chicago? Leave Leigh-Everett to screw-up on his own." While proceeding with stew and bread making preparations, Hester tried imagining what it would be like returning to the bosom of her Romani relatives.

Finally she sighed, and proclaimed decidedly, "Hell with them all."

Her thoughts returned to domestic activities and the excitement surrounding having visitors. Sidney and Nadya were the last, and what a disappointment they'd been. A movie film crew was decidedly different, that was for sure. She kept LC's master suite, with the huge four poster, and sitting seat at the end of the bed, always in ready. That Sydney fool had loved it, especially the two big closet-like things and all those old dull rugs. She would let Leigh-Everett decide if the lady or the producer should have that room. Especially since it had its own bathroom, and he said she was dirty from falling in that silly Logan lady's root cellar. That picture caused Hester to laugh aloud which in turn caused Dobie to awaken for a moment and look up to make sure her great treat-giver was okay.

Then there were the two bedrooms down the hall the other way that shared a bathroom. She also opened up a bedroom on the other side of the stair landing. She kept them all clean and dust free just like her mother Hester before her had.

Fool Leigh-Everett was darned lucky to have her.

Then out of the blue—quite suddenly and inexplicably— Hester felt immensely lonely.

Another mess. Margaret Deer's thought was accompanied by a hardly audible sigh. *And* with her friends involved yet again.

And, she'd have to face Leiv, Glover, and Apply without letting on, that she knew anything. Holding her tongue last winter about Naomi had been hard enough.

Now, Mary and Elizabeth-May.

This time, her sigh was loud enough her fluffy black cats—Samara, nestled comfortably in her lap, and Silky stretched out on the deck at her feet—looked her way with the combination of loving curiosity and disdain only felines can pull off.

It was building into one of those smokey sunsets—she speculated a fire somewhere west or south of Shiné combined with some windblown-sand dulled the horizon's brightness while simultaneously intensifying the colors. Not that Margaret knew of any particular fire, nor could see any actual particles in the air, or smell a telltale odor of smoke. But the absence of glare, and uniqueness of the reds and blues from among the many sunsets she'd seen, told her the truth of the matter. Hermit Chan would know for certain. He was a connoisseur of all matters of Mojave light—sunset and sunrise. The smell that laced the evening air was one of full-blown spring. Not quite fully blossomed into the unmistakable and pollen-laden aroma of June, but no longer early desert spring air for sure.

There's nothing I can change. Margaret Deers took a deep breath, taking it all in, and let her eyes rest upon the horizon for several quiet moments. Indeed, she continued to find her expansive wooden-railed porch ideal to take in her view of Shiné. Similar to Leiv's place, her vista was panoramic, but from a different angle. Both their properties were aeries, but hers was west-facing, while Rhodes Castle looked toward the east. She'd pointed out to Leiv on several occasions—and using quite flowery language—he saw the morning light as it first touched Shiné, while she enjoyed the brilliance of fading-light sunsets across a seemingly infinite desert horizon.

Unfortunately, though trying very hard to accept her current dilemma, Margaret's mind wanted to return to the knowledge Leiv and her son Glover didn't have. Knowledge either or both of them might eventually ferret out—so why not tell them what a bastard Mary's husband was. And that before Tony died of natural causes, some guy had come looking for him. She was sure Elizabeth-May had taken matters into her own hands.

"What will Leiv and Glover do when they find out?" she asked Samara and Silky aloud. *Especially Leiv.* Hard to walk away from information like that when you've been a judge all your life.

His father Everett had been fond of saying "way back when," how some people had moral compasses, and some didn't. Everett's attribution for his comments was to LC. A man of many sayings. She laughed from the knowledge of all the witty, un-witty, earthy, and sometimes just plain stupid quotes attributed to Leigh Cooper Rhodes. *Well,* no one could deny he had built a town alright. But what kept her admiration alive for the man, wasn't his town-building feat, or his collection of sayings. No, it was what she knew to be his love for his wife, Viola.

As was her habit, Silky turned over on her back, stretched her legs straight up, wiggled around as if scratching a back itch, while making a low rolling guttural sound. Margaret fancied she was conversing, and in answer said, "You want to know what I think will happen when Leiv figures it all out?"

This time, Samara, still sitting comfortably on her lap meowed quite loudly and in a plaintiff air which was her specialty.

"I really don't know," Margaret admitted.

Tonight was their weekly get-together at Leiv's in the Castle's withdrawing-room, as LC called it. She was extremely fond of getting together with Pastor Apply and Leiv, and a couple months back, Glover also started coming when he could. Even when the fireplace wasn't lit, and with Dobie preferring to hang around more and more with HM, the ambiance was still one she found lovely—yet hard to explain. She guessed it was *partly* the type of furniture LC and Everett had acquired, and then the couple pieces Leiv added contributed, *partly* the fragrance of whatever finger food HM chose to prepare, and *partly* the aroma of Harvey's Bristol Crème, or Bailey's B&B—the liquors Leiv insisted on serving. She wasn't much of a drinker, but the Bristol Crème at least was sweet, and she was developing a liking of the stuff.

For the first time, a possible ambiance explanation came to her. *It's the booze that makes me feel so relaxed.* True or not, liquor was an easy and convenient explanation.

Finally, her mood lightened for real. Despite the knowledge heartbreaking secrets and revelations regarding her two friends were inevitable, words she'd used more than once describing Shiné evenings came to her: *La nuit*. The night, *a beautiful time in Shiné.*

Then Margaret, the keeper of many secrets, gently nudged Samara off her lap, got up and went inside to prepare for going to The Castle. Tonight she would see her friends—and hopefully Leiv's new movie-making acquaintances. Glover had called her and mentioned the possibility. Maybe it would turn out to be a rather festive event? *I think I'll wear my long denim cowgirl-skirt with the embroidered roses around the hem.*

Chapter Two

The Longest of Days

From LC's journal: Love sitting in my withdrawing room talking with Viola, and the boys running around with those wooden guns Jules carved for them. A man couldn't be happier in this place Viola created for us. Do tell though, heard some interesting things in this room. Just sitting around listening.

Saturday Still

Hester was almost surprised, but not completely. Something—she had no idea what—told her to look up from her kitchen worktable where she was sprinkling shredded Asiago as the finishing touch on her miniature-quiche *hors d'oeuvres.* Consequently, when David Milhouse appeared in the doorway of her kitchen-kingdom, she caught him in her peripheral vision exactly at the same second he appeared.

This "forewarning" was an unusual experience for Hester. In her mind, seeing the future, reading palms, and all that other rigmarole was just plain silliness. No matter what her Chicago relatives thought. Some of them even making money using such "gifts." Still, Hester could not ignore she sensed *something.* Her solution was to pretend it didn't happen.

83

On top of the "knowing" he was there, Hester also felt a tingling sensation she hadn't experienced since childhood—and during those trips back to Chicago with her mother. One memory in particular; the day she first laid eyes on Andreas Herne, her distant cousin and only lover. Now dead at the hands of Kizzy Lovel, she was sure. *Yep*, it was the "tingling" sensation of a besotted teenager. A recognition not as easily brushed aside or ignored as second-sight. She certainly didn't like the feeling, not as a young girl, not as a grown woman, and especially not right now, right here in Rhodes Castle.

But there he is, standing in my kitchen, and me feeling so funny.

"Can I help you with anything?" David asked.

Hester couldn't believe how nice his voice sounded—even though she thought his accent kinda snooty—nasal like. *Not from Chicago, and definitely not from the Mojave.* She belatedly realized, he was probably from LA, and it was just a movie-type way of talking. Clearly, it was thinking about her wonderful Andreas and that *bi-lacho* Kizzy getting her all confused. Dulling her brain.

David took a few more steps into Hester's domain without waiting for an invitation. "I mean, all of us descending upon you out of nowhere. Probably a lot of extra work for you." He sniffed the air loud enough for her to hear. "And it really smells great in here. The whole house really. Your bread aroma is everywhere."

She didn't look up from her *hors d'oeuvres* to meet him eye-to-eye.

"Mr. Rhodes told us you were from Chicago. You know, I'm from there, too," he added. Then David repeated his complement, "And it really does smell great all over..," he waved one arm in a sweeping gesture, "...here. I was going to say 'the house,' but this place certainly is more than that."

"Castle," Hester heard herself provide the appropriate word. She also noticed her earlier yo-yo-like funk had completely disappeared. *Talks funny, but he's from Chicago, too.*

*   *   *   *   *

Doctor William "Will" Walker was excited and pleased Leiv had called and again invited him to The Castle for the evening. He was well aware Leiv hosted a regular "thing" in LC's withdrawing-room every Saturday evening—and though often invited, especially since Glover started attending—he usually declined.

Doc Walker preferred stretching out in his *own* well-padded recliner—with a *modest* fire going in his *modest* fireplace; then purposely and quite enjoyably lose himself in his latest medical journal. He thought it imperative to "keep-up," and subscribed to four or five publications. His favorites were JAMA, BMJ, and The New England Journal of Medicine; and though they were available online, he still liked print versions the best. There was something physically pleasing, while simultaneously intangible in turning and reading real paper pages. He was reluctant to give-up the experience, and had yet to start receiving issues on his computer or tablet. *If I ever will.*

Nonetheless, his journals would have to wait. Tonight, he not only eagerly accepted Leiv's invitation, but also arrived early. *I need to know the latest on Mary Jones.* Indeed, he was very worried for her.

Had he really seen a hand last night? Her hand? It was dark, his eyes older and less sharp at night than he would like to admit, and he'd had a couple. Indeed, it took three shots of Johnnie Walker Gold at TGS Tavern before he screwed-up enough courage to walk down Shiné's Main Street. His goal—to tell Mary Jones how he really felt about her. Will knew Leiv and Glover were being pulled into Mary's spell—but to his mind, they were just mesmerized by her uniqueness. *I'm actually in love with the woman.*

He sighed lightly, but no one present seemed to notice. It turned out to be one of those rather dark and "otherworldly" nights. Indeed, some nights in Shiné were darker than others, and Will knew this because he did a study. Admittedly, *not exactly a study using the "scientific method,"* but he took notes on an almost nightly basis for five years. Kept a precise and detailed handwritten log using a pricey astronomers' nighttime light-monitoring gadget. And his hypothesis held fast—some nights were darker than others, regardless of moon phases, star visibility, or season. When William explained his findings to Hermit Chan—he immediately agreed.

Some things you just know, William thought from the moment he first made his fledgling observation years ago. He was a man of medical science, and knew himself to be in most things, logical, methodological, and a follower of facts. Yet, when it came to dark nights, William was quite aware his initial belief was weird and other-worldly. Closer to a matter of conjecture in the realm of science fiction, rather than a scientific hypothesis. *I could also feel the darkness.* It was a craziness he could not let go of—being a medical doctor notwithstanding. Hence, the evolution and completion of his data collection.

Last night on Main Street, looking up at Mary's balcony, it was very dark, too. And he was rather tipsy. Was it really her hand? *No, it was Max's.* That's why he'd yelled, "Leave her alone, you bastard!" So Mary would step to the side.

He put his Shiné-logo cup with nothing but the dregs of some very aromatic and tasty hot chocolate on the side table to the right of his armchair. Most of Leiv's guests were drinking Harvey's or B&B—but tonight he needed the sober comfort of old fashioned cocoa.

Then there was the uncertainty about what next. Should he, or should he not talk to Leiv or Glover—*maybe both*—and tell them what he knew? Even though his 911 call was directed to Shiné's Chief of Police, and he and Glover talked at the scene—he hadn't mentioned the hand either time.

William wanted to sigh aloud, but held it in and made sure his congenial, slightly smiling public-face was solidly pasted on. He'd been a doctor for many a year now, and knew "dead" when he saw it. *Then last night, Mary came running out...* William held back a shudder remembering. *Horrible.*

For a second, he wanted to get up—leave, run, go home. Escape and take solace in his own chair, or even fiddle around in his home-office. Both places would be better than here and dealing with how he felt about Mary. He would be safe there at home. *Here*—though very comfortable and enjoyable on other levels for sure—was enemy land. *Why had I wanted to come in the first place? To confess what I saw maybe?*

With the passage of a few more seconds, and out of the blue, he wondered what it would be like if Mary Jones were sitting in the armchair across from him, next to Pete, instead of Marilyn LeBlue. *No,* he shook his head slightly—his movement imperceptible, he thought, to any of Leiv's guest possibly looking his way. Besides, they—he, Pete, and Marilyn were at the end of the circle near, LC's gigantic fireplace. Too far away for Leiv or Glover to see. *I've been a bachelor for so long now.*

His mind went back to the pavement in front of *Le Bric-à-Brac* on main street last night. The body—*Johnny Max's body.* He found two first names annoying, but held back his emotional criticism. *The man is dead, no matter how movie-star-fake his name sounds.* And with that thought, his mind seemed to quiet, his mood lighten.

But then he thought he heard the music-lady sitting across from him say something about working with Johnny Max?

Marilyn's comments drew Leiv from his observation of Doctor Walker. Something was on the Doc's mind, he was sure. His friend seemed caught up in his own thoughts—serious thoughts if the look on his face was any kind of gauge. Leiv even thought he saw Doc shake his head—but he couldn't be sure from where he was sitting at the top of a grouping HM had rather artfully, he thought, arranged for them to all fit in LC's withdrawing-room.

But his attention quickly shifted to Marilyn LeBue when he caught her use Johnny Max's name. Since arriving at Rhodes Castle, Leiv knew from HM, Marilyn had showered, then bathed after her initial shower, showered again, and finally taken a nap. Seeing her now, devoid of root cellar detritus, he took in for the first time the reality Marilyn was an attractive woman. Indeed, he found her face pleasing in a traditional sort of way, while also emitting a unique quality.

Like my Melissa, not just another pretty "face" in the crowd.

He even liked Marilyn's fall-back facial expression—even when talking about what was clearly an unpleasant experience, anger or malice didn't mar her expression. He liked that. *Another trait in common with my Melissa.*

"Johnny Max," Marilyn was saying, "was a bastard, and that's for sure." Her tone was surprisingly soft, given the import of her words. "Did two shows for them on his stupid show on a stand-in basis—needed the money at the time. I certainly was glad when the regular Sound Editor got well." She shook her head, sucked in air, and in a modest display of emotional distaste licked her lips slightly, as if the memory of those experiences still left a foul taste she needed to get rid of. "I'd had quite enough of the bastard by the time I left that show."

Glancing around quickly, Leiv took in that with Marilyn's mention of Johnny, she had grabbed everyone's attention, not just his. The Music Director quickly brought her right hand to her mouth in a femininely-charming gesture, and said, "Ooops." Her gaze was in Lloyd's direction. "Sorry about my language, Padre. And I am sorry he's dead." After a few seconds though, Marilyn amended her apology, "Especially for Mary's sake. But he really wasn't a nice man at all." She was sitting in a burgundy Victorian replica Spoon-back armchair next to Pete Lily to the left of the fireplace. One of several chairs Glover and Pastor Lloyd—under

HM's direction— had brought together from various spots in LCs withdrawing-room to form a semi-circle to accommodate both Saturday night "regulars," and his film crew guests. Pete was sitting in the chair next to her.

"And all that happening while we were looking at the chimney." She shivered.

"Well, actually, it happened last night. Before you came to Shiné."

Lloyd nodded affably in response to her Padre apology, and smiled. "I've heard much worse." His smile morphed into a chuckle. "Right here in this room." The pastor's tone quickly turned somber. "But it is horrible about him falling off Mary's balcony like that." Then he shook his head, and added in afterthought, "I'm not a priest, by the way."

Leiv turned sideways in his own chair in time to see his friend bestow on Margaret Deers a pastoral-like smile. Margaret was sitting in her regular Saturday night spot on the love seat, perpendicular to Leiv and Lloyd ensconced in their identical armchairs. To her left, she would ordinarily have a clear view of LC's "Stone-Monument" fireplace. Tonight, Marilyn and Pete in their high-backed Victorian armchairs, cut off her fireplace view; but the arrangement definitely provided for easier conversation.

"And," Lloyd added, turning his attention back to Marilyn, "this Johnny Max must have been quite an unpleasant character for you to pick-up on his hatefulness in such a short period."

"Ha," Pete scoffed.

"Ha, indeed," Charlie echoed from his spot on the opposing loveseat to Margaret's, and to Leiv's right. "You never met him."

"Two first names…," David quipped quietly from his spot next to Charlie.

Leiv thought David's *sotto voce* comment sounded like a mumbling meant only for himself; but when Leiv looked over at David, he caught him exchanging a knowing look with Charlie.

Evidently they were of like minds when it came to names. *Or*, a little voice in the back of Leiv's head speculated, *shared a secret known only to them?*

Leiv took a sip of Harvey's Bristol Crème, and looked around. In general, despite feeling like today was becoming the longest-of-days, Leiv wanted to smile. *LC would be pleased*, he thought. A spring evening still cool enough to build a fire in his prized fireplace, a collection of interesting people along with some good friends, a nice glow to the room—and the aromas of bread, appetizers, and liquor coloring and flavoring the air. Then looking down as if contemplating his aperitif glass, Leiv actually surreptitiously looked around from under his eyelids a second time.

It is a nice gathering, he reaffirmed.

A rather contradictory and unsettling thought he recognized, given today's events. Two bodies, maybe murders, and finding a book he and Glover were scared to open because of the age of the binding and paper. After checking with Forensics in both Needles and San Bernardino, they'd already been instructed to take "the book," currently locked up in Glover's safe, to a museum specialist in Vegas tomorrow—making sure chain-of-custody was documented. Although, the book certainly looked in good shape, given it had been wedged in that chimney for at least a decade or more. Glover had insisted on following instructions. "I'm not about to take any chances. Not unwrapping or opening this thing until an expert tells me how to do it." Now, at this moment, Glover was looking at his mother and smiling.

Must be the atmosphere. Despite the day's happenings— and in contrast to LC's withdrawing-room's shape, its old-world furnishing, and specially selected accoutrements—there was also a "camp fire" feel to tonight's gathering. The movie crew was dressed casually—jeans, Dockers, chambray or Henley shirts— and Leiv was glad he chose at the last minute not to don his customary smoking jacket. His outdated affectation, though connecting him fondly to LC and a period in time his grandfather was fond of, would not have been appropriate tonight. And Margaret's choice of western skirt, though quite feminine, blended right in with his around-the-fire construct.

Pete was carrying the conversation forward, "Two first names or not, the media loved him." He shook his head in seeming wonderment. "Johnny Max did some pretty awful crap."

"Like what?" Glover asked, leaning forward in an armless parlor chair he squeezed in between Leiv's armchair and the end of Charlie and David's loveseat.

Pete didn't answer immediately.

Leiv had wondered earlier why Glover didn't decide to sit next to his mother, instead of next to him. But watching him now, he understood. *For the advantageous perspective of taking in the whole group.*

Their entire circle: Charlie and David on the loveseat to Glover's right, then Doc Walker in an armchair with LC's fireplace behind him and slightly to his right, then Pete to the other side of the fireplace, Marilyn next to him in an identical chair, then Margaret with a loveseat to herself, before coming back around to Pastor Apply and himself in their matching armchairs—directly facing the fireplace and completing the "camp fire" circle. HM's elaborate *hors d'oeuvre* and bread spread sat enticingly on the tables in front of them all. Various drinks were on the sideboard behind Margaret.

Once again, he offered mental kudos to the Chief of Police for placing himself so strategically, and to HM for organizing and preparing such an elaborate spread. And on darn short notice. *Of course it is also our dinner, too.* Leiv also amusedly invented a not-present Walker Johns in his temporary position as deputy—standing beside and slightly behind Glover taking notes. Just like on Elizabeth-May's property earlier.

In the real world, the eager and accommodating Ambulance Tech cum Special deputy Walker Johns had volunteered to stay at the office. Making phone calls. Pushing and pulling on friends and contacts to get lab and research results moved through fast. Leiv planned on making sure Glover dropped off a "goodie-plate" for Walker if the "campfire" didn't breakup too late.

After a couple moments or so of thought, Pete finally said, "Don't imagine you spend much time reading the tabloids?"

"Well," Glover admitted affably, "I do buy groceries. They're hard to miss standing in line."

"One of his 'misadventures'—as he called them—did involve a civil suit." Pete looked away a few seconds, as if recalling the incident. "What I remember is he was drunk, no way he should have been driving. And there were serious injuries to a young woman. I think she recovered, but not sure—"

"Crippled for life." David's voice was flat, but Leiv heard underlying censure, maybe even contempt. "'Misadventures' my butt. Then there was the prostitute he beat up."

"Oh yeah." Marilyn's voice was now more emotion-laden—pure animus was evident. "She didn't press charges. Paid her off, my guess."

Charlie was not to be left out, "And his ex-wife—I can't remember her name this second…"

"Mary Jones," Marilyn readily supplied.

Once again, Leiv was abashed. *Everyone knows who Mary Jones really is.*

"Yes. Well, a lot of their divorce acquisitions got leaked to the press," Charlie continued. "Some of it pretty awful."

Leiv asked softly, "Physical abuse?" He couldn't imagine, and wasn't sure he wanted to know.

"Physical and mental was the gossip I heard on the set." Marilyn sighed as if dredging up Johnny Max's villainy in detail was taking its toll. "Nobody liked him. Both set and cutting-room people were always talking about him."

"What about management?" Glover asked.

"You mean like the producer and his gang?"

Glover nodded.

Marilyn shook her head. "Once they hired me, never

much saw them." She chuckled slightly. "I don't play golf." Then she gave Charlie a little smile.

With his peripheral vision, Leiv saw Glover fall back into his chair. And though he didn't actually turn to his right to look at him and see what expression was on his face, Leiv did wonder what Shiné's Chief of Police was thinking. *Solid motive for Mary as Johnny Max's killer?*

"Where's the deputy?" David asked.

Before Glover could answer, Leiv lied, "He couldn't come. Tonight is family night at his mother-in-law's. And this weekend is southern fried chicken. Not something to be missed."

"Smart man." David smiled. "Family connections and duties are not to be brushed away lightly."

Charlie leaned forward a bit and looked at Leiv directly. "How did you manage to combine old-world ambiance with—" he asked, paused, then after hesitating for a few more seconds, finished with, "the desert esthetic?"

How much should he say? That this larger-than-life room's purpose was suggested by Viola? A room his grandfather started calling the "withdrawing-room." *Pompous and folksy at the same time.* "It was my grandfather, Leigh Cooper Rhodes, that created this room," Leiv said. "My father, Everett added some touches."

"For example," Leiv elaborated—caught in the moment of remembering. "The chair frames were original, purchased by his grandfather in the nineteen-forties, then my father Everett had the leather and cushion-stuffing replaced in the sixties." He patted the side of his armchair seat. "And still comfy."

"And that fireplace," Leiv continued, then paused and waited for Charlie to follow his gaze, "I call grandfather's stone monument."

Pastor Lloyd Apply added, "I've always heard that's what LC called it, too."

Then desiring to stop journeying farther down memory lane, Leiv asked, "How is your evening going, Will?" Leiv hadn't forgotten the earlier looks on the Doc's face. Looks he still didn't know how to interpret.

"Dark is the night, and cold is the ground," Will mumbled.

"Blind Willie Johnson," Charlie said a tad louder than Will, but in a similar low-key introspective tone.

Leiv didn't know what they were talking about, figured it was religious, but before he could get clarification, HM came in carrying a huge dish. Apple cobbler by the smell of it. And once again, he was amazed at all the celebratory treats HM had prepared. *She must have been cooking all day.* The aroma was heavenly, and memories wanted to come — eating memories with Melissa. But he refused to go down that path. *Not now.* No matter how powerful the pull of apple-cobbler aroma.

"Had this in the freezer," she said contradicting his cooking-all-day guess.

David stood up quickly and said, "Here, let me take that."

Quite amazed, Leiv watched as HM did something he would have never considered in her repertoire of emotions. Hester Miller blushed while David took the massive dish of cobbler from her. "Would you join us?" David asked her. "I'll serve if you like."

She seemed momentarily speechless.

"Tell you what," David offered before anyone else could comment, "Why don't I dish us up a couple servings, and I'll join you in the kitchen."

"You don't have to leave—" Leiv started to offer.

Hester quickly cut him off. "I'd like that." Then she was gone in a flash, and David followed within a couple short moments — balancing two dishes of cobbler while somehow managing to open the heavy and massive withdrawing-room doors before anyone could get up and go help him.

She left as quick as a shy young girl. Leiv realized his mouth was hanging open slightly and he quickly closed it. *And David, acting like a hormone-driven teenager.* A quick look around revealed none of his friends who also knew HM—Glover, Lloyd, Margaret, Will—seemed to be as surprised as he was. Leiv did see what he interpreted as an amused look on Pete's face. HM and David Milhouse—definitely a surprise. Then he caught himself. *And why not?*

Then Leiv watched Doc Walker as he got up, walked around his armchair to the sidebar behind his chair and refilled his diner-style mug with hot chocolate from a thermal carafe. "Sure you don't want a cordial?" Leiv called out.

Will turned toward Leiv long enough to answer, "Not much of a drinker you know."

Leiv thought he heard more in that simple statement than the words might indicate, but let it drop. *Something is going on with Doc.*

A close-by cell phone hummed loudly from vibrating. Glover's next to him? Before he could say anything, Margaret said, "Turn the damn thing off, for goodness' sake. You're off duty."

Leiv was surprised Margaret not only heard the phone from her position on the loveseat, but also recognized it was Glover's. But again, before he could say anything, Pastor Apply spoke.

Looking at Margaret, Lloyd said, "Sometimes, My Dear, duty can't be escaped."

Just like with the Doc's words, Leiv thought he again heard more than the *words* in what the Pastor was now saying. This time though, Leiv was able to identify sadness edging his friend's words. *And weariness, maybe? Not easy being a pastor,* he thought. *Nor a doctor.* Two friends with burdens he speculated.

A comfortable silence fell upon the gathering for a bit— everyone seemingly caught up in private thoughts and speculations. *Or maybe just taking time to enjoy their food and drinks?* He'd devoured two pieces of bread and three mini-quiches already.

The withdrawing-room door again opened, and HM reappeared, but this time more in character, she announced in her patented being-put-upon tone, "Phone for you Leigh-Everett." She had a portable receiver in hand, and had clearly returned to her traditional demeanor. "You want to take it in here?" Hester's expression clearly indicated she didn't want to walk over and bring him the portable receiver. "She insisted she wanted to talk to you personally."

"She?" Leiv asked.

"That crazy woman at that funny-named place in town."

"Mary? Mary Jones at Le Bric-à-Brac?" He stood, walked around their camp-fire circle, met Hester near the door, and took the portable phone. "Thank you," he said, and followed her back out through the withdrawing-room double-doors into the hall. Yet, he closed the door very slowly—torn between wanting privacy to immediately talk to Mary, and not wanting to leave yet-to-come conversations.

Behind him, he did hear Glover answer his cell phone, "Yeah, Walker, what's up?" And as he inched the door closed behind him, Leiv was sure he also heard Charlie's voice asking something about a church altar….

Pastor Lloyd Apply felt his stomach sink when he eavesdropped enough to know Leiv was talking to Mary.

Today had been a tough one from the start, and it wasn't getting any better. He was a Pastor, and consequently used to members of his flock pouring their hearts out to him. But this afternoon—despite his past experiences over the years—had not been a joyous one. First Mary in town, then Elizabeth-May at her home.

I'm not a priest. Indeed, no vows or Code of Canon Law were directing his behavior. His "flock" nonetheless, expected confidentiality on his part when they opened their hearts—and for some—their souls to him. But now, with all these nosey film people, and Leiv and Glover hanging around digging for the truth, he was very worried. It was one thing for Mary and Elizabeth-May to make their peace with God through him—but the law was an entirely different thing. *And Leiv is a former judge, no less.*

Pastor Lloyd Apply *wanted to* sigh. *Wanted to* go home. *Wanted to* say a special prayer at his church's special altar. Then he *wanted to* bury his head in his big fluffy pillow on his bed and tuck his quilt in tight.

As if reading his mind about his altar, Charlie White asked him directly, "What's this I hear about you having a most spectacular altar in your church?"

Pushy LA types, Lloyd thought, and didn't immediately respond. He also wondered if there was more to this man than appeared. With further thought, he also speculated Charlie White was angling for taking pictures in his church—or worse, a follow-on film about Shiné Community Church.

His hesitancy evidently didn't deter the producer. Charlie continued, "I hear it's pretty big with a three-panel sculpture across the front?"

Lloyd continued to remain mute on the topic, and wasn't sure exactly why.

"I hear it tells the story of Gethsemane, the Crucifixion, then rising from the dead."

Charlie had finally succeeded in capturing his attention, and in response Lloyd opened up and told Charlie and anyone else listening—David for one seemed interested—the story of how LC and Violet had Shiné's Community Church altar commissioned way-back-when.

After hanging up with Mary, and then stealthily looking around to make sure the foyer was empty, Leiv slipped outside through LC's stained glass front double-doors—heading to his

Athol hideaway.

He wanted some time to think—commune with the night. It was too dark to go the distance of trudging up the hill and around back to LC's secret cave. Indeed, in a complete emotional turnaround, the thought of being inside again was no longer appealing. He didn't even want to escape to his library and see the moon through his special office window, even though he knew from looking up, a beautiful sky awaited his inspection.

No, he needed to be outside, smell the night air, "feel" the Spring evening. Though dark, it was still fairly early, and his guests wouldn't miss him for a few moments. A time to assimilate today's happenings, and especially the call he just received.

Her voice had been soft, inviting. "Can we have breakfast tomorrow morning?"

Leiv had nodded though he knew she couldn't see him through his cell phone.

"At The Greasy Spoon?"

He'd nodded again.

"I'm guessing you're nodding," she concluded in a laughing tone.

Leiv finally said, "Yes. I'd love to."

He would return to his gathering soon—after the effects of Mary's voice wore off. Indeed, this particular Saturday night gathering had turned into quite an affair by his assessment. More interesting than most he hosted since returning to Shiné a couple years back. Even better than many of the black-tie events he was forced to attend in Chicago or Springfield. On top of that—HM had outdone herself. *The warmth in the room, the aromas.*

Here outside, it was colder than he expected, and there was a dampness to the air that made him shiver— and for the first time, Leiv realized he was becoming tired. Still, he wasn't in a rush to go back in. Probably being with Apply, Doc Lloyd, Margaret, Glover, and his film-crew guests, had been invigorating—masking the real length of the day and its occurrences. Leiv figured later, when they all headed to their various bedrooms, he would probably want to flop dead-tired into bed.

For now, he walked toward the front Athol-stand that provided a substantial hedge to the west side of the front door and the Castle's circular driveway. The trees, some twenty to thirty feet away from the house itself, formed a tree-wall that made an amazingly private sitting area behind them. The feeling when sitting there wasn't exactly like a bench in a maze, but one could easily imagine one. *Especially if you're a kid.*

The "kid" in LC had built around the huge trees, making sure they weren't damaged. And Leiv still remembered the day LC's and his own father Everett had the teak English garden bench delivered "from somewhere to their west." Everett had supervised the workmen in the particulars of an exact placement of the special bench—as to maintain privacy among the trees, but close enough to the house to afford a view of night skies above the trees. Wanted or not, Leiv still carried an emotional attachment to that bench from those remembered days. LC was still alive then, saw what his son had done, and knew his grandson would enjoy.

"You sit on it first, Leigh-Everett," his father had said. It was the first night after the bench was in place. Then his father held his hand while they watched the night stars together. Leiv felt a lump in his throat—*even after all this time. Not now,* and as he was about to turn away, push back memories, change his plan and go back to his Saturday night gathering—a voice behind him said, "I waited a minute or so after your Pastor's altar story before coming out to join you."

Leiv wasn't able to check his startle-response in time, and physically jumped. *Charlie White?*

As he turned to face the film producer, Charlie added, "Thought maybe you were having an assignation with someone. I didn't want to destroy your moment."

"Assignation?" Leiv chuckled lightly, giving himself time

to let the anxiousness Charlie's surprise appearance generated float away on a light breeze that seemingly appeared from nowhere and swept lightly through LC, Everett, and now Leiv's outside-alcove of sorts. "You sound like me." *Using words from several generations.* "Old school speech."

"And snooty and affected. Right?"

"That's one of things you have to watch out for in movies, right? Language suiting the period?"

Charlie nodded and took a few steps toward the bench Leiv was planning on retreating to—*alone.* That is, before he decided to go back in. When he realized Charlie was planning on staying, Leiv quickly adjusted his plans. There might be some advantage to talking to the movie-maker in private out here. Indeed, the whole film business was turning out to be more interesting than he initially thought.

Leiv followed Charlie and sat down next to him, and oddly he thought—the bench was still warm from the day's heat. After a few moments of easy silence, Leiv said, "You know Hermit Chan...I mean Douglas...once told me he could smell the difference between a night sky and a morning sunrise. He claimed the air was different."

"I like him," Charlie said. "Though I think he lied about knowing where that chimney was." Charlie shook his head. "And I don't know why."

Maybe because he knew about the notebook? Or the body even? Leiv kept his thoughts to himself. "They don't call him Hermit Chan for no reason I'm told."

"Were you told by your friend, Chief Deers?"

"I'm guessing you don't really know that much about me. But I've only been in Shiné a couple years now, and I've relied very heavily on people like Chief Glover, Pastor Lloyd, and Doc Walker for filling me in on a lot of stuff.

"'Stuff?'" Charlie repeated the word with teasing emphasis.

"A 'technical term,'" Leiv said.

"From your days on the bench?"

Leiv laughed again, but he did wonder how Charlie knew he'd been a judge. *Somebody blabbing to the producer no doubt.* "'Stuff' as in hard evidence if you're talking about my judicial days. I was referring more to Route Sixty-six, Mojave Desert, and Shiné 'stuff.'" Leiv smiled from generalized remembrances of in-chambers conferences on evidence.

Charlie slouched down a bit, stretched his legs out, and looked skyward. Not as tall, thin, and lanky as his photographer Pete, he still wasn't a diminutive man, and Leiv imagined once dressed-up in movie director clothes, Charlie probably presented a striking presence at film festivals and premiers. Not that he followed movie-land happenings much, but Margaret occasionally mentioned items—Johnny Max for example.

Leiv followed suit and stretched his own legs out, crossed his ankles, then also looked up to a twinkling sky above. He asked, "Do you know which constellations are which?" But before the producer could answer, Leiv changed subjects. "Was Johnny Max really the slime-ball Marilyn and your team portrayed him as?"

"There you go again."

Leiv again heard teasing amusement in Charlie's tone—similar to how Glover sometimes interacted with him. And surprisingly, he felt at ease with Charlie. Not annoyed, or protective that his ego was being tweaked. Comfortable. *And I hardly know the man.*

Charlie continued, "Slime-ball. Haven't heard that term in ages." His gaze was still directed upward. "As to your second question, I only met him once. And do you know how you want to take a step back from someone?"

"Repulsed." Strong word he knew, but it was the first one to pop out. However, Leiv didn't feel like confiding how he'd often experienced such loathing with some defendants. The ones he knew from day-one were evil. *Ones that sometimes got off.* The law was the law, no matter his feelings, and he had been sworn to uphold it. *And then there were the ones I would have liked to shield from the law if I could have.*

As it turned out, "repulsed" was evidently the word fitting Charlie's experience. "Exactly," Charlie said. "And, no, don't know doodly about the stars except it's very nice how they seem to shine extra brightly out here. Pete says it's because of the darkness. No ambient city light to dull their sparkle."

"'Doodly' was for my benefit, right?"

"Yep. With you, it's old fashioned, if not archaic words." Charlie tsked lightly. "And with your Chief of Police, it's western terminology."

Leiv smiled. Still, he wondered how Charlie White was picking-up on everyone so fast? Part of being a good producer and director he guessed. That would explain an interest in Shiné Community Church's altar if he'd heard correctly on leaving the withdrawing-room. Wanting to film there he guessed. Then unbidden, an entry in his grandfather's diary came to him almost verbatim: *"I'm having my altar, don't give a darn if Reverend Armstrong has his britches all bunched up. Altars make a church. And a church, a tavern, and sidewalks make a town. Viola will prevail with the church and sidewalks…but I'm thinking…the tavern is up to me."*

Following his remembrance, came a scary thought. Could Charlie White possibly know about the Mojave-Stones? *No,* Leiv decided emphatically. The producer didn't know about the Mojave-Stones—*no one* knew about the Mojave-Stones except himself.

No, it wasn't knowledge of the stones bothering Leiv about the producer. *But there is something.*

Chapter Three

What a Difference a Day Makes

From LC's journal: Sometimes you look one way, and stuffs happening the other way. Gotten tricked like that many a time. Thank'ya God, my Viola was looking the other way for me when it really counted.

Sunday

No matter how old he got, Leiv was still surprised how different he felt in the light of a new day. Even after a day like Saturday.

He thought hopefully, *probably just going to be another clear blue-skied Shiné day.* Nonetheless, he didn't get up from his desk and walk over to the library window to confirm his supposition. The sun had technically risen while he worked at LC's library desk. The "work" in question was sitting and thinking about how good the French toast he'd planned on making would have tasted. *Not this morning;* he would be eating out. Yesterday happened and his world changed forever—not just his breakfast plans for this morning. *But so much easier to think about missed French toast.*

Leiv took a long deep breath of what was surprising chilly and dry air for inside, and rolled his head from side to side, then back to front—trying to consciously relax his shoulders. Accompanying the head-rolling, he heard in his inner-ear a couple bones crack, and figured that wasn't good. *Too tense.*

It was Sunday morning, and his habitual morning question of *"cupola or library?"* was answered after waking up at 4 A.M. when he couldn't go back to sleep. Copula won the first spot. Consequently, when he started this Sunday in pre-dawn darkness, he'd already peered upward into a still dark sky from the Castle's Pentagon Copula, seeing stars and a couple what he guessed to be planets. Just like when gazing up into last night's much darker sky—and not knowing if he'd seen Mercury, Venus, Jupiter, Mars, or a yet unidentified twinkling star or planet. He and Charlie had both been star-challenged. Nonetheless, as galactically ignorant as he remained in the dawn of a new day, whatever he saw was gorgeous. *One day I'll get smart on that planet stuff.*

Today was not that day. *Today* he needed to go into Shiné town proper. Leiv wondered how he would feel seeing the sidewalk in front of Le Bric-à-Brac again. *If I go that far down Main Street.*

He pulled his mind back from Johnny Max's dead body splayed on the sidewalk yesterday, with Glover in his solitary stiff and stoic looking stance. *A praetorian guard of sorts.*

"As if Shiné is anything like Rome," Leiv bantered aloud to himself. Which took his mind back to French toast of all things. From the start when Leiv moved back to Shiné, he insisted HM take Sundays off, and he would prepare his own breakfast. He imagined Sunday mornings were a lonely time for HM since her mother died, and at first, he also insisted she keep Dobie with her. That was no longer a question since Dobie hung out with HM all the time now—without his encouragement.

His lingering "being alone" empathy for HM was based on personal experience. It was a long time after losing Melissa before he was free from fighting minute-by-minute depression. Now his heartbreak and longing came in waves, at unexpected times, and often prompted by unexpected events.

Ninety-nine percent of the time on Sundays, Leiv prepared French toast for himself—his egg batter rich with cream, sugar, and sour cream. He almost salivated, but caught himself in time.

Also these days, after Sunday breakfast, and while most of the Shiné population was in church listening to Pastor Lloyd Apply's words of wisdom, Leiv preferred to take the time to reflect in private—either here in the library, the Castle's copula like earlier this morning, or secreted in the semi-darkness of LC's secret cave.

As for this Sunday, Leiv wondered what his friend would be talking about from the pulpit? Two deaths in town was quite an event.

Leiv further reflected that Sundays, all the way back from and through his childhood, were "special." Not that he had ever attempted to "characterize" a Chicago Sunday evening or morning, or a Springfield sky, or any other darned sky he could remember. *Or contemplate the spot I wanted to watch a sunrise from.* He laughed into the silence of his grandfather's office. Partly, at how his world had changed in the last few years; partly, at how he had changed.

"It's your fault," he said aloud again, this time as if he could cross the years back to LC. These meanderings back to his grandfather's world were a recurring phenomena Leiv was starting to call "The Shiné Effect." His grandfather pulling him into the Mojave with him—though not yet swallowing him up—but causing him to look at this desert in a different way.

Leiv's thoughts inexplicably moved on to helicopters, and he shivered without thought. Now that he'd met the man, Leiv easily imagined Pete Lily flying in a helicopter, taking pictures from above. A very unique perspective, another different way to look at the desert. Indeed, Leiv almost wanted to experience what

Pete had yesterday morning, looking down at Rhodes Castle. But not quite, not in this real world. Heights and helicopters were definitely not his "thing."

While indulging in his wandering thoughts, Leiv was also doodling circular squiggles on a yellow-lined notepad placed in the middle of his desktop. His writing implement was a newly sharpened, right out of the box, wood-cased number-two lead pencil. He'd taken it from one of several boxes he recently found in the back of LC's hideaway cave. Looking down, taking in and realizing what he was doing—again involuntarily—his fingers started rubbing the yellow painted wood-surface of his pencil—and an intense desire to go right then to LC's cave and commune with his grandfather swept over him.

Not now. He commanded himself. *Maybe later today.*

In half-an-hour he had an appointment to meet Mary Jones at TGS. When she'd called last night, pulling him from his "party," he wasn't able to refuse her request. Not that he didn't want to see her—more that he was scared to.

His fake antique French rotary phone surprised him once again with its loud and demanding ring. *Just like yesterday.* Indeed, just like Saturday morning, it was Chief of Police Glover Deers on the other end.

While waiting for Mary at TGS, Leiv couldn't stop his thoughts from revisiting his meeting with Margaret Deers just a few months back. Winter it was, and as was her wont, Margaret had settled into her special booth in The Greasy Spoon, pretty much disappearing from front door sight. It was the farthest away high-back booth—near the door to the restrooms—with her back to the front door. Location, booth design, and choice of booth seat, shielding most of its occupants from prying eyes. She called it the "hideout booth." No one wanted to sit there—no view. Margaret had wanted to thank him for saving Glover's life.

This morning, without thought after parking in TGS's empty parking lot, Leiv had walked in, chose the same booth, sat down, and waited for Mary to arrive. He'd come early on purpose, even though it required pulling himself away from the comfortable cocoon of his library office and doodling inspired thoughts. Driving the few miles down a paved, but usually forsaken-feeling road wasn't such a big deal anymore—but having to face Mary again after yesterday—he wasn't sure what would happen. Good or bad. Looking back, talking to Margaret that day in the past had been so much easier.

And I'm still hungry. Missing his French toast was still a sore-point. He knew some of Chef Jack's lunch and dinner creations were on par with anything he'd ever eaten, even at some of the swanky places in Chicago or New York. At least there was hope for good food soon.

On cue, "Haven't been in for awhile," Chef Jack said, heading his way across the three or four feet from the kitchen door and his booth.

"My loss, Chef." Leiv smiled. Not only did he think Jack was a culinary master, he also liked Shiné's only chef. Something about the look and feel of the man, just made him want to smile. For a second, Leiv thought of his bailiff way-back-when in his first courtroom, his first stint on the bench—Purnell Bracken. His name came to him in an instant, *even after all these years*. Many a day, Mr. Purnell—as he was called by all—helped Leiv survive. Even this morning so many years later, sitting in the back-booth of TGS, Leiv blanched, remembering some of the mistakes he almost made in those early days—except for the grace of Purnell.

"By yourself?" Chef Jack drawled. Leiv almost laughed, but caught himself in time. Sometimes the Chef favored him with an exaggerated "Noo Yawk" accent, and other times with an east-Texas drawn-out and quite lyrical drawl. He had no idea why— or if Chef Jack actually had an accent of any kind.

"Mary Jones is joining me." Then Leiv remembered the car he saw. "Your lot is empty, but I thought I saw a car parked on the shoulder by that stand of Athols just before arriving at The Greasy Spoon."

"Broken down maybe? Waiting for Henry from Pump and Fill next door to get there?"

Leiv made a face. "Could be. Hadn't thought of that."

"Besides, how can you hide out here?" Jack shook his head. "You can see for miles in all directions."

"Yeah," Leiv agreed while thinking about what he thought he saw. "There aren't that many clumps of Athols around. You have to plant and water trees if you want them." Even though Jack was staring at him, Leiv closed his eyes for few seconds, re-visualizing where he saw trees recently. "There's a clump at Elizabeth-May's, just growing wild right before her driveway."

Leiv heard the front door open, and now with eyes wide open and looking at Chef Jack, he watched as an adoring smile spread across the chef's face. But Jack, evidently remembering Leiv's presence, quickly turned his countenance into a non-emotional mask. Leiv turned and stretched so he could sneak a peek around the booth's view-blocking-post to see who had entered and ignited such adulation from his favorite chef.

Mary Jones was heading their way, directly toward the back booth. *She knows instinctively where I am.* She was wearing a hug scarf and sunglasses, putting him in mind of a bygone Hollywood era. Leiv almost smiled at her movie-star pretense — given they were *in* TGS, *in* Shiné, *in* the middle of the Mojave. Ironically however, he belatedly realized, Mary had a classic movie-star look to her face, that scarves and sunglasses weren't capable of hiding.

Jack leaned down a bit and said *sotto voce*, "Horrible about her ex falling off her balcony like that."

The fact news traveled at lightning speed around Shiné was not a surprise to Leiv. But Chef Jack *also* knew who Mary Jones actually was, and the body was Johnny Max, her ex-husband. Once again, Leiv's pride was pricked. *First Glover, the film crew, now Chef Jack...what a fool I am when it comes to women.*

Except for Melissa of course. They fit.

To cover his pique, and memories of Melissa that wanted to resurface, Leiv asked in as nonchalant tone as he could muster, "By the way, I don't see it on your menu, but do you make French toast?"

Mugs had great binoculars. He'd been choosey when purchasing, comparing several top brands—actually doing research on the computer at the library. Not something he often did. *"Leave no footprints,"* a phrase his Uncle Harry often used. Of course, Uncle Harry would have been appalled by the Internet.

Finally, Mugs selected a Canon with multi-coated lens and the ability to adjust to his screwed-up left eye. He actually ordered it through a local camera shop in the neighborhood. No Internet kind of trail for anyone to follow. Shelled out a load of money, *but boy, was it worth it.* Paid cash.

But this clump of trees, right in the middle of nowhere, and just where he needed them, was a real stroke of luck. Luck was not something he counted on. *Smarts* was what Mugs prided himself on, like with purchasing his binoculars. Nevertheless, even with his good hiding place and great binoculars, Mugs wasn't sure who he was looking at when she first got out of a small brown older Nissan pickup truck. The lot was empty except for the castle-owner guy's pickup, which he'd parked in front of the door. For some reason the woman parked way out in the last space near the edge of the diner. But then as she walked toward the restaurant's entrance, he whispered to himself, "Yep, that's her alright." The wife of his second target, Johnny Max.

Trying to fool me. She was wearing an oversized babushka, like an old-timey movie star hiding from photographers. In Mug's mind, she made a stupid move where she parked—*brought my attention to you.* Though her appearance was still a surprise, and he wondered if she was connected to the castle-guy inside—or to Anthony L's book? He couldn't imagine how.

Well, she certainly wasn't smart like him. He was staked out in a perfect spot. *And nobody knows I'm even in town anyway.* Showed the difference between pros and amateurs. After watching for cars going by all the time while getting settled, Mugs had eventually gotten out of his car and taken a position in the crux of two of the trees. He didn't like these desert pine trees. Sharp, and one branch that brushed his mouth left a salt residue. Remembering, he reflexively rubbed his mouth and chin hard with the slender long fingers of his left hand—though he *was* grateful for the foliage coverage.

Even so, Mugs's overall desert-appreciation-mood hadn't improved much since leaving Elizabeth-May's property. *Nasty desert trees*, he irritably but half-heartedly griped while swiping at his mouth a second time. The ugly edge to his mood, despite his appreciation of his smarts, and despite his tree-coverage luck, was mainly because here he was, yet again, hiding and waiting because his timing had been off. *I must be slipping in that department.* Not a fact he was yet willing to admit.

He shook his head and whispered, "No way. It's Anthony L who's screwed this all up. Dying like that on his own. And then putting that damn book in the chimney. And now here I am, paying the price." Realizing he was arguing with himself, and aloud, he allowed himself a small chuckle. *Nobody around to hear me.*

Mugs further placated his irritation with himself by remembering he was known for his patience, found it usually paid off, and served him well. Still, he should have grabbed that silly-looking old woman before that film crew got there. Now either that damn hick-cop or his sidekick had the book. He had to do something. You didn't fail with his bosses.

Then his mind reverted to the woman wearing the babushka—Johnny Max's wife. Then to Johnny in particular. He had it all figured out how he would take Johnny out, and that was the very next item on his list.

His cell phone vibrating in his pants pocket stopped his murder-plan musing. He pulled it out to see who the hell was calling him. Only one person knew where he was, and what he was doing—his current employer, Lucky's kid, Doc Francis.

It was a typed message from the Doc. Mugs rolled his eyes at what the world had come to. *Text messages.* Then he read what it said: "Good job making it look like the woman."

"What the hell is he talking about?"

Mugs sorely wished for the old days. The old ways. Then for a few seconds only, his mind flitted back to a comfortable spot in time—the days in his grandmother's backyard with nightshade growing all along her back chain-linked fence.

Then he scratched the back of his neck, allaying a feeling someone was watching him. He looked around. *Nothing. Of course not, no one knows I'm here.*

Hester was making bread again. The film crew was still hanging around, and they seemed to really like it. *David in particular.* In line with her mother's ways, as she did yesterday, like she always did—Hester tried to start her dough early in the morning while her kitchen domain was warming up. Somehow the aroma of fresh bread seemed to help with the house-warming process. Her kitchen, the whole Castle actually, got cool at night—winter and summer. "All the tile and bricks," her mother had explained when showing her the ins-and-outs of housekeeping. *A long time ago now.*

When the phone rang, Hester had just finished measuring all the dry ingredients for a batch of rolls into her large industrial quality mixer—so the timing wasn't that horrible. Still, the noise irritated her, and since she'd watched Leigh-Everett leave, she wanted to catch the call before one of those LA types took it on themselves to answer.

"Yes," she said brusquely into the receiver. Dobie, stretched out this time in front of the warming oven, lifted her head for a second, then was back to sleep before many more seconds passed.

The call was from Needles Deputy Sheriff Brad Temper. She liked him. Hit her as plain-spoken and down-to-earth—not like puffed up Leigh-Everett and his buddy Glover. Although, she didn't think Shiné's Chief of police was all that bad at his job; it was just when he was with Leigh-Everett, the two of them acted like they knew secrets nobody else did. Brad was in Shiné and wanted to know if Mr. Rhodes had left yet to meet Chief Deers across the street from the sheriff's office at Le Bric-à-Brac?

After a quiet sigh, Hester deigned to tell him what she knew—"Leigh-Everett left at least an hour ago."

She almost didn't tell him the rest of it about what else happened when Leigh-Everett left. After all, it wasn't in her nature to blabber on about suspicious happenings or premonitions, now was it? But things were changing since meeting David—in ways she wasn't sure of, or necessarily liked. Besides, why should she care about Leigh-Everett anyway—he was a fool, now wasn't he?

Nonetheless, she told Brad about the car she saw earlier pulling out from behind the Oleander hedge at the turnoff to come up the driveway. It was a-ways-away, but she was sure she saw a small white sedan pull away from the end of the Castle's driveway *before* Clueless made his way down the drive and headed toward town.

Okay, Brad mused, he was used to Hester Miller's abruptness—bordering on rude, but who was he to judge? Who knew what her past held? On top of that, she was local, sort of. At least for two generations.

With those thoughts in mind, he was not prepared for her

supposition somebody had been watching and waiting down by the beginning of the Castle's circular driveway, behind a clump of Athols no less. Indeed, the Deputy Sheriff was not only surprised she would be watching and mention it to him. He was also amazed she could see so far. *Eyes like a hawk no doubt.* But then on second thought, he figured not much happening around that place escaped her notice.

She stated her concern quite clearly and forthrightly, saying, "Right before Leigh-Everett left, a white sedan kinda car pulled out headed toward town before Leiv. Like they was watching for when he started to leave, then was following him from *in front* of him."

He knew what she meant, and it was the technique of a savvy follower. Quite believable in a big city, but here in Shiné? Thinking about what she said, he shook his head. Yet, he was interested, and wasn't about to discount what she'd seen. *Nope, been a Deputy Sheriff far too long to discount anything.* But it certainly was a different Hester than the one he thought he knew. In addition, there was something about her words "small white sedan" that wanted to trigger a remembrance in his brain.

He drove over from Needles immediately when Glover had called yesterday. It was a straight shot once he got to the interstate, and a fairly easy drive after that. *Not that long really* — and he was driving a newer fully equipped white Crown Victoria everything worked in — *and it didn't smell.* His new cruiser even had a pricey new light bar. And once he got on the interstate, it was usually "smooth sailing." He could even turn on his new roof mounted red and blue flashers and mostly go in the fast lane if he had to.

Truth be known — *but not shared with anyone* — sometimes he liked coming out to the desert over hanging around in the city. And after awhile, if stuck out in the Mojave long enough, he just didn't want to rush back. Not that Needles qualified as a "metropolis" by any means. *But out in the desert is different.* And this investigation in particular, he found interesting.

The first forensic team had come and gone, and he wanted to talk to Glover again personally before heading back himself. The crime scene across the street was still taped-off, and a newbie Needles Deputy Sheriff in an unmarked vehicle was left to keep an eye on Mary Jones—where she went, what she was doing. *Tanya*, he shook his head again, mentally thinking his deputy's name. Brad knew he was old fashioned in that way— but he still hadn't adjusted to modern female deputy names. Though, to his continuing chagrin, he could still remember, and felt his face warming with the memory, a bar fight he'd been in several years back where a sumo wrestler-sized drunk was disparaging in unnecessarily vulgar terms he didn't now want to recall even in thought—that any man named Brad couldn't be taken seriously. A fight had ensued. A *good* fight in his mind— with him on the winning side. He and a couple deputy-friends had been reprimanded. Brad smiled, then sighed—amazed at his own contradictory psyche when it came to deputy sheriffs.

Admittedly, he didn't like Shiné's makeshift overnight facilities. The Chief of Police's back of the office "cold room," was a makeshift morgue, *kind of,* and holding cell, *kind of,* and overnight sleeping quarters, *kind of*—if you weren't squeamish. The fold-up cot's mattress was only marginally better than the floor, and the emotionality of the place sucked. And there was that time a few years back when two dead women shared the room. He even remembered their names, Naomi Hall and Georgie Oakes. He shook his head yet again, this time in amazement at how Glover—he knew with a whole lot of help from Leiv—pieced all that together last winter.

He *did* have a long-standing invitation from Margaret Deers to overnight at their house whenever he wanted. But something about staying in the same house with The Chief and his mother seemed odd.

Having considered the ins-and-outs of his head-shaking and sigh-producing situation this morning, Brad took a long deep breath, and looked out onto Main Street from the Police Office's front window. *Glover's window to Shiné.*

"I do like it here for short periods," he told the empty office. "But how Glover and Leiv stand it all the time is beyond me."

There was a shower tucked away in the farthermost corner of the cold room which he'd used in the past. He always carried a spare uniform and toiletries with him. San Bernardino was the largest county in the United States—twenty-thousand plus square miles if he remembered correctly. Never knew where he might end up.

"I guess I better go shower." He wanted to be ready if he got another call from his Captain in Needles, especially with Glover somewhere at the moment unknown, and Deputy Tanya Cramer across the street at Le Bric-à-Brac. He was hoping his department had picked up the trail of Mugs Nightshade from Chicago—last spotted at McCarran International Airport in Las Vegas. They'd lost him in Vegas, and he'd sent Glover a flyer.

"That's it," he said, again speaking to an empty office as he walked over to the corkboard behind the coffee paraphernalia. There it was, in black and white, the Sheriff's commentary on the bulletin board printout, "*...surveillance pictures showed a man registered as M. Paulina, at a rental company Gold-Level user fitting Nightshade's description picking up a pre-assigned white Toyota sedan in their rental self-serve parking area....*"

Instincts born in experience and in Brad's cop mind said he couldn't take the time to take a shower no matter how much he wanted to. Or wait for temporary deputy Walker Johns to arrive to man the Chief's office. Even though he knew Shiné's ambulance technician had a heavy foot—time was of the essence. He looked up at Glover's wall clock and was surprised to see it had been awhile since he had talked to Hester Miller.

On his way out the door his cell phone rang. It was Tanya informing him she followed Mary Jones to TGS. She was currently, "Just watching, figure she has to eat. But thought you might want to know." Then before he could press his "call end" button, she asked, "What kind of car is that Nightshade character supposed to be driving?"

Leiv wasn't quite ready to leave yet, even though Glover might be outside waiting for him already—though he doubted it—it was more to the Chief's style to blow his horn when picking him up. Here already or not, horn or not, Glover could come in if he wanted. He needed another cup of coffee before leaving— more accurately, he needed *time* to think. *Time* to digest his latest encounter with Mary Jones.

Neither he or Mary had eaten their French toast platters. And while Chef Jack took their plates away to put in take-out boxes, Mary took the opportunity to theatrically, he thought, replace her scarf and sunglasses disguise, then rush out while the adoring-chef headed to the kitchen—leaving Leiv in a muddle of surprise, sadness, and anger at the unfairness of life. He was also still hungry.

Mary had dropped a metaphorical bombshell he didn't yet know how to handle. Indeed, she shared with him a piece of information he couldn't imagine sharing with anyone else. *Ever.* But then, there were those meddlesome-little-issues like duty, justice, procedure.

Chef Jack returned, put two take-out cartons on the table, refilled Leiv's cup, and palmed the thirty-five dollars Leiv had placed on the table for payment and tip. All accomplished fluidly, silently, and swiftly. In a very few minutes, the chef was back in his kitchen making banging sounds. TGS was empty other than himself, so Leiv was sure Chef Jack recognized his expression of confusion, and desire for solitary thought on his face. *What a gem,* he thought while simultaneously dropping his putout feelings forever toward the chef for also knowing who Mary and Johnny Max were.

Mary's words took center stage in his mind.

She'd leaned across the table toward him, her voice low and unhappy. "Why JM just appeared like that—" She had shaken her head. "Out of nowhere." Then Mary relaxed her shoulders a bit, her eyes shifting from staring at him to some spot on the wall near the men's restroom door. "We got into an argument. Didn't take long. Not unusual."

Leiv thought her tone of voice and delivery were more like she was talking to herself. While re-looking at the scene last night—a scene she'd participated in.

"Somehow we carried the argument outside, onto my little balcony." She had looked to him for confirmation of some sort. "I guess we were yelling pretty loud." She paused. "And JM was waving his hands around a lot."

Leiv had waited for Mary to continue when she was ready. In truth, he felt an inexplicable touch of fear that kept him silent.

"Then I heard him yell from down on the street. 'Leave her alone, you bastard!' Again Mary paused.

Again, Leiv waited.

"Surprised, I jumped a little and looked down. But I know my balcony." She took in a long slow breath before continuing. "JM jumped more than me, you see." Her eyes came back to Leiv. "And he lost his balance, and fell off." She shook her head as to negate that night. "And I felt so dizzy myself. Light-headed, like I was going to pass out." She took another breath before adding very softly, "It was awful."

Then Mary grabbed her scarf, retreated behind her glasses, and fled from TGS.

Remembering, rehashing, regretting what he now knew, Leiv rubbed his eyes. Hard. But he couldn't make what Mary just said go away.

Mugs pulled out and headed toward town. His gut told

him they'd be heading toward Fifteen, not Forty, and the expert he was at following from-in-front-of, he headed north. He was sure the castle-guy was planning on hooking up with the cop guy in town—and they would then have the book.

Anthony L's stupid book will soon be mine. Then he would take care of Johnny Max. *Idiot actor with two first names.*

In passing, he did see the nose of a car on the bar-side of TGS as he headed away from the restaurant, but it was too quick of a sighting, and the car was parked at the wrong angle for him to tell what kind it was. Definitely not a cop car, though. *No need to worry.*

He just needed to find a nice spot past town to wait to get them in his sight. Then pull out ahead, then the ambush when they least expected it.

When Glover finally arrived and honked his horn, Chef Jack offered it was fine for Leiv to leave his pickup in TGS's parking lot.

Leiv had not ridden in Glover's cruiser often, but when he did, each time felt like a unique experience. One time in particular—he still retained residual emotion from riding from the Summit Restaurant with Glover and SBC Deputy Portia Sherman. He was in the back seat feeling like a criminal being hauled off to jail. With Glover and Portia in the front seat playing at being professional—while undeniably flirting.

Not that riding in a cruiser was totally unfamiliar in his life. Before Shiné, way back in Law School, one of the class requirements was called Police Ride-Alongs. Later, when on the bench, his still friend and ally, Chicago Captain Hal Herman ended up including him in a real pursuit when he was on a stakeout that turned active. He was just supposed to see how it felt to sit all night in a cruiser. Not see real action. Leiv *still* remembered that dark Chicago night. *Still* remembered the rush—and the fear.

This morning he was riding shotgun, and the fanciful part of his brain imagined he was a cop on duty with Glover. A reality check reminded Leiv he never was a cop, but a sedentary judge. And most importantly, in their current situation, they weren't going after bad guys; just heading to Vegas to get an old deteriorating book looked at.

Desert terrain was growing on him, and it promised to be a pleasant drive. What at first seemed like endless stretches of uneventful sandy-colored dirt, had on closer inspection revealed to his eye a surprising number of plant species. He just hadn't taken the time to look. It would also be an emotionally easy drive, *except for passing the turn off to Lookout Loop.* Then once on I-15, the short leg into Vegas would be the easiest part. Especially in a cruiser in the fast lane.

He still had them in his rearview mirror. Sure looked and felt like they were heading up higher down the paved road and his lay-of-the-land memory told Mugs they would be on the Fifteen in just a bit. He didn't like that, wanted to do this where it was still flat, but a good spot had not materialized.

He got dizzy up high. For a moment Mugs flashed back to the view of Chicago he took in from the top of the John Hancock building before leaving civilization for this awful place. On top of that, once on the interstate, it would be harder to follow-from-in-front. *I need to end this now.* He pulled over and prepared to do what needed to be done. Wouldn't take long, he could see their car getting closer. *Easy target.*

It happened fast, on the stretch before the freeway, right after passing the empty car. *Broken down, gone for help,* Leiv thought the moment before it happened.

Leiv didn't know if he heard the crack of the shot first, or felt the front end of the cruiser pull to the side and hit shoulder first. He did know Glover cursed. He tried to speak, but nothing came out. Leiv also thought he heard Glover say for some reason, "Front wheel drive."

Then Leiv was upside down, feeling almost like he was hanging from his seat. Then his head hit something sending a searing pain through his forehead. He grabbed for anything he could get hold of, then another shot, which he was sure hit the cruiser again. Still, he couldn't speak or steady himself.

From some direction he heard Glover curse more vehemently.

It felt like the cruiser rolled some more, and they were now on their side he thought. Then the sound of a seatbelt unbuckling? He wasn't sure.

Not sure of anything anymore. Though Leiv did think he saw a glint of sun on metal, and hoped Glover had managed to un-holster his Glock.

"Get out," Glover hissed from his left. "Tank's been hit."

Leiv tried to do what Glover told him. Make his hands work. But nothing. His head hurt even more, and he couldn't speak. *Maybe I've got a concussion?* Then he lost track of Glover and thought he heard more shots—a barrage actually. His brain was working, but he couldn't seem to keep his eyes open. He knew he was about to pass out—and felt ashamed that he was. *I'm no help for Glover.*

Glover and I have been shot at again.

Then someone was pulling on him. Dragging him. Almost like when he was stuck in the bramble at Lookout Loop. And though Leiv could hear, he could no longer seem to open his eyes. Couldn't see to do anything.

"Got to get you out of the car." The voice was male, he thought, and strained. *Is it Brad? Can't be.*

*   *   *   *   *

When Leiv next opened his eyes, he was lying on a mat and with the blurry but quite attractive face of a female paramedic staring into his eyes. "What happened?" He barely heard the whisper of his own voice. "Is Glover alright?"

A male voice close said, "Of course I'm alright." *Glover.* "You can't get rid of me that easy." From his voice, Glover seemed to be sitting or squatting on the ground next to him.

The shots were so close, so real, so many. "I thought…"

"You thought we were both going to die." Glover's voice was surprisingly sober, in fact upbeat given the circumstances. As if everyday life was in progress—not that they were just ambushed by someone wanting to kill them. And been in a car-rollover.

"Yeah. I thought you were dead." His throat hurt but he could still hear the sound of his own voice. Feel the emotion he hoped was not coming through in his voice. *Too old for this.*

"Brad pulled you out, you know," Glover said. "The shooter got back in his car and took off when Tanya, then Brad arrived. Walker is at the office, coordinating with State and County."

Tanya?

"Even with the three of us, we couldn't stop his car with just our handguns. They went after him—"

Then everything went blank for a bit.

After he didn't know how long, someone took Leiv's hand. It felt good, soft. "Well you're both alive and we'll be taking care of you." The paramedic's professionally cheery and upbeat tone immediately brought him back into the world of the living. Next she was shining some kind of beam of light into his eyes. "Paramedic Walker Johns before he headed to the police office recommended we take you to the hospital for observation. Possible concussion—"

Paramedics here already. Walker Johns and a lady I don't know?

"No way," Leiv declared as emphatically as his throat and weak voice allowed. With both arms and hands he forced himself up into a sitting position. He felt dirt and stones cut into his palms from the pressure of his weight and the effort. *We must be on the gravel shoulder.* He could also now make out a stretcher on the ground next to him. He figured he was on a mat, and they were getting ready to lift him onto the stretcher. *No more hospitals for me*, his psyche insisted. His hospital experiences last winter were still too fresh in his emotional memory-banks.

Vaguely, he heard a phone ring, *a cell phone?* Glover was still there, just more to the side, and pulled something out of his pants pocket. *Yes, a cell phone*, Leiv assured himself. It was suddenly important he was experiencing the real world accurately.

No concussion, no off the deep end, no hospital for him. While Glover talked into his phone, Leiv took the moment to attempt looking around and getting better bearings on where they were and what the situation was. He caught in the corner of his left eye the tail-end of Glover's Police Cruiser—engulfed in a plume of black smoke on the shoulder behind them. *Totaled*, he guessed. Leiv was also sure paper pages were swirling all around them—airborne and flying across the highway and beyond. And very close on the ground, the smashed remains of several takeout containers. *French toast this Sunday morning was not to be.*

"Brad's got sight of his car," Glover informed him and the paramedic. His words were almost swept away by the same Mojave out-of-nowhere freaky wind gust that was taking their precious book away.

The wind's suddenness and sharp impact brought with it more clarity to what just had happened. *Deputy Sheriff Brad Temper saved my life.* Leiv attempted to sit up straighter, this time using his legs to help. He needed to get up, get more information, help Brad and Glover. And Tanya? While he struggled physically, and before he could get anything else out of Glover, a car came to a screeching stop about two-hundred feet on the shoulder in back of them and a parked Medivan he just noticed was there. *Of course, the medical technician hadn't just appeared from nowhere. Got here fast. Miracle workers.*

The car was a dark blue Volvo station wagon. *Lloyd?* Within seconds it seemed, Lloyd jumped out of his car heading toward them. Glover quickly stood and simultaneously headed toward Lloyd.

In an attempt to follow Glover, Leiv again used all his physical resources. He needed to stand. It hurt like hell and Leiv felt like he might topple over—but he forced himself, made his body move. *I have to do this.*

The ambulance tech tried to grab him, but she was too late. Leiv caught sight of her name badge when she reached for him. *Annie.* Indeed, his first step—more of a lunge forward, was a shock, and his legs almost gave; but *darn it*, something was happening and he planned to be part of it.

"Judge Rhodes, you have to go to the hospital." Annie's voice sounded incredulous Leiv wasn't taking her advice. "Concussion," she demanded.

"What's going on," Leiv tried shouting to Glover's back. Searing pain shot through his chest.

"What's going on," Lloyd was also shouting at Glover from the other direction as they both hurried toward Glover from their separate positions.

Leiv so wanted to run, to join them quickly, but his legs just wouldn't move faster. He tried to yell out, "What about the book? We're losing the book…." He guessed his voice was hitting air as barely a whisper.

He could hear Glover saying, "Lloyd, we've got to head out to catch up with Brad and Tanya. You can see my cruiser is totaled. Brad's put out an all-points. We'll have to forget the book...."

Lloyd seemed at a loss, but quickly recovered. Leiv figured something in Glover's eyes must have indicated the importance of the situation. "You drive. Keys are in the ignition."

Through pure will power and pain tolerance, Leiv was now close enough to the two men to think he saw a glitter in the Pastor's eye.

Push, he demanded of himself.

Leiv still felt dizzy, but like Lloyd, also excited—finally, and quite miraculously, he found himself half running, half stumbling toward Lloyd's car. He managed to open the Volvo's backdoor and insert himself in the car's backseat before Glover fully comprehended what he was doing and object. He was proud of himself for getting this far given every part of his body now seemed to ache.

Still, he was able to take a few seconds to wave out the window at his guardian-angel medical technician and yell, "Thank you. Not to worry, Annie, I'll be fine." It sounded to his ear more like a whisper, but she must have heard him because her response was to put her hands on her hips, shake her head, and wag an accusatory finger at him. Though, he thought he detected the slightest of smiles—but wasn't sure.

On the driving front, before Lloyd could object, Shiné's Chief of Police was gunning the pastor's pride-and-joy heading North toward I-15, Deputy Brad Temper, and a would be assassin. Leiv barely had time to buckle himself in and he could feel his heart beating hard and fast.

I don't care about my heart. In fact, he almost smiled in thinking about being in the backseat of an aged Volvo, during a police chase, in the middle of the Mojave desert, with an equally aged Pastor riding shotgun—and him, feeling on the edge of passing out.

Shiné, what a place.

Chapter Four

What a Difference a Morning Makes

From LC's journal: Sometimes you look one way, and stuffs happening the other way. Gotten tricked like that many a time. Thank'ya God, my Viola was looking the other way for me when it really counted. Don't know what Viola sees in me. Don't know why she loves me. Don't make sense, but she sure does.

Sunday still...

He had seen them perform their amazing aerial dance before, but Leiv was still mesmerized by the synchronized avian-ballet.

This was maybe the third or fourth time since he arrived in the Mojave that Leiv was lucky enough to see their dancing flight. He watched now—almost mesmerized—as a sizable flock of small blackbirds rose *en masse*, switching back and forth several times in a swirling pattern, up, then up some more in a soundless tornado-like, yet exquisitely graceful vortex. For a second he was tempted to make the exceptional move of opening his library window so he could hear the wind-rushes he knew from past experience were taking place. Just seeing them was almost not enough.

Leiv didn't get up from LC's desk though. *Too lazy? Too worn out after everything that's happened? Too dopey from Will's drugs?* He wasn't sure, but seeing the black birds again reminded him of Elizabeth-May's—*more like Anthony L's*—betrayal-insurance book pages swirling away into the wind while he was sprawled helplessly on the side of the road.

It was late afternoon now, he was home at last, back from chasing an elusive would-be assassin to no avail. *Sequestered* in LC's library.

At least he, Brad, Lloyd, and Glover were alive and well. He'd also met the new and quite sharp Deputy Sheriff Tanya Lewis. Also on the plus side, in the end he hadn't been forced to go off to the hospital in Vegas, Barstow, or Needles. *Another bullet I've escaped.* Leiv shook his head for what felt like the umpteenth time since arriving home and becoming cocooned in his library sanctuary.

This Sunday, from its early morning start until now, remained unbelievable on many levels. On the time front, much had slipped away—but the slice of this morning where he dragged himself to Lloyd's Volvo—continued to replay itself in Leiv's brain in slow motion. No painful detail missed.

Fortunately, he actually wasn't in much pain now. Chef Jack driving his truck and Doc Walker following, had most kindly, he thought, brought his car home from TGS. In the process, Doc also picked up antibiotics and pain pills from the pharmacy. And once at the castle where Glover had unceremoniously dropped Leiv back home, Chef Jack—under the instruction and watchful eyes of Doc Walker, and the equally intense put-upon glare of Hester—had cleaned and poured liberal amounts of anesthetic on his abrasions and cuts. Fortunately, the sting of that treatment was long gone. The doctor also cautioned him about the possibility of concussion and infection from his abrasions.

"And if you don't want me to send you to the hospital, you better do what I say," Doc Walker had instructed quite firmly. "Hard-headed. Both you and Glover."

Remembering, Leiv smiled slightly, then realizing nothing on his face now hurt from the effort, thought, *good drugs.*

"And I'm checking you out again fully tonight," the doctor also insisted, "when I come back." He said the "come back" part edged in either dread, or fear, or sadness. Leiv couldn't figure out which, but then was not the time to pursue further. Doc Walker next turned to Hester and said, "Make sure he gets plenty of rest and plenty of liquids with the antibiotics I'm leaving for him."

Amazingly she'd nodded agreement, though at the time, Leiv found it hard imaging HM as a nurse-like caregiver. But in coming in the room, she'd locked his library door behind her and said firmly, "No wandering filmies coming in here." And a pot of hot tea and his pills distributed in a plastic pill box now sat on the corner of his desk.

She turned to leave, saying as she did, "You're not to be disturbed."

But then he stopped her. To take a moment, *no, to make a moment.* There were two ladies he needed to talk to tonight—and he would start now, here, with HM.

"Hester," he said, not yet sure exactly what words he was going to use.

After Hester put the tea tray down on the library desk, and as she was turning to leave, Leiv said her name, "Hester," as if he wanted to tell her something.

Since stealing the Mojave-Stone from his library safe over the winter—*from right under his nose*—she hadn't felt comfortable being in there with him around. However, when she turned back,

Hester hoped the smile on her face was pleasant enough. *Don't want to betray anything.* Admittedly there had been the day when she would have reveled in her theft. Somehow things were different now; but she wasn't quite sure how. Or why.

"I was hoping you'd stay a moment, join me for a cup of tea."

What is he talking about? The only times she could remember of them sitting down together were in the kitchen. And those "chatty times" hadn't been many.

Hester didn't stop moving toward the door though, and for a moment, she questioned whether she heard him correctly. Then she realized her continued movement toward the door was to make a comfortable distance between them in what she knew to be his special library place. With Dobie, she knew what to expect. With Leigh-Everett, that was a different matter. Who knew what the fool was about to do?

She turned back to him. "I have a lot to do in the kitchen," she said in a softer tone than she expected she would.

Somehow, he seemed to understand her discomfort. "I'm sure Dobie will be missing you soon. She relies on you a lot these days."

"She's old," she acknowledged. "And tired." *Maybe I am too.* Quickly, she banished the aberrant thought.

"At least she's spending what's left of her life happy here with us. With you," Leiv said with what sounded like a touch of sadness, which surprised her. Not so much that he missed Dobie—she figured he would, maybe even liked that he did—but recognition of her feelings had actually been a consideration to him.

Still, she straightened her posture and lifted her chin. "Don't have time for tea."

"I want to talk to you about the Mojave-Stone."

What? her brain screamed. "Yes?" she forced her tone as neutral as she could. Her legs felt weak. "I'll sit, but not long." She looked around as if being in his office was actually strange to her, then sat on LC's aged and rather rickety Queen Anne style armchair. The chair was positioned at an angle to his desk—its mauve-colored re-upholstery, initiated by Everett, was now thin and faded almost to the point of non-existence from the years taking their toll. She'd sat in that very chair when Leiv's father, Everett, was still alive; the thought offered her a modicum of reassurance.

Leiv took a deep breath, looked away out what she called his "precious" window for a moment, before starting what he wanted to say. "My cousin Nadya—your friend, right?"

Surprised, and at a loss, Hester could only nod.

"Well," he sighed again, which gave her a few seconds to compose herself for what might be coming. "She's been telling your relatives she stole the Mojave-Stone."

She felt her eyes widen, her pulse quicken.

"Thing is," Leiv swiveled his chair so he was facing and looking directly at her. Then he leaned forward slightly and spread his hands. "What Nadya gave a Mr. Bersch to return to me—I think I have the name right? Well, what she gave him is fake. Not a real opal at all."

How could this be? Hester wasn't sure what expression was on her face, but her mind and emotions spun. She needed time to figure out what Leigh-Everett was telling her. What was a lie, and what was truth.

He turned from her, his gaze reverting back to his window. *That damn window, that damn Mojave opal.* At least he was waiting, giving her time to take in all the levels of truth, subterfuge, and intrigue he and she were unraveling, and simultaneously still hiding.

He was speaking again. "My guess," he continued, "is while she and Sydney were visiting she broke into my office safe and stole what she thought was the Mojave-Stone."

Hester inhaled a sharp breath, *I can't believe it,* and she couldn't help herself from shaking in Leiv's wake of revelations. "How could she?"

"Sneakily, Mr. Bersch said. She waited until we were all asleep and crept in here and stole it."

Hester felt several moments pass while she gathered her thoughts. She looked down at her hands. They were calm at least, clasped together firmly, but not rigidly in her lap. Then Hester shook her head—while unbeknownst to her except for a feeling of her cheeks warming—a look of amazement spread across her face. "She was a sneaky one, that one." *He must know I had to be involved. Even as clueless as he is.*

"Sydney has filed for divorce. Abandonment," he added. "Though the current terminology might be 'desertion?' Haven't been in Illinois in awhile now."

"He was—" Hester stopped herself mid-sentence— now was not the time to reveal what an idiot she thought Sydney was. "And I'd liked her." *The daughter I never had.*

Hester cleared her throat dramatically, and asked firmly and rather loudly, "So, are you saying the Mojave-Stone doesn't exist?" She hoped the flicker of doubt seeping into her brain didn't show in her eyes.

With one of what she considered his stupid smiles, Leiv answered without seeming hesitation or second thought, "Of course it doesn't exist. There is no Mojave-Stone."

After Hester left, Leiv sincerely hoped he'd sent her off— free to fly with what he imagined was the exhilarating abandon his blackbirds displayed. Fanciful he knew, especially given Hester's personality.

Still, he persisted in imagining her metaphorically flying around, seeing the world outside of Rhodes Castle. He smiled with the thought, *even a former judge was allowed an occasional waddle-around in sentimentality—wasn't he?* He had no firm idea or conjecture of how it would happen—but in his heart, he knew Hester Miller II needed to be *free* of the Mojave-Stone legacy.

Indeed, *free* of Rhodes Castle. How he would manage running things on his own, he would think about later.

After she closed the door, rather softly he thought, Leiv decided he need to "talk" to his grandfather before tonight's gathering. Maybe re-read sections of his journal he almost now knew by heart. He would go to their special secret place. *The place* where LC kept his real diary, not the fake one left in the library for HM to discover. This secret hideaway, only LC, Viola, and Leiv knew about.

From his assigned Rhodes Castle bedroom window, Charlie watched Pete as he prowled around the area south of the circular driveway—his camera hanging from his shoulder. Charlie couldn't help himself. Admittedly, spying was easy for him, but he was mainly watching because PL sent out some kind of infectious artistic appreciation vibe he enjoyed trying to also experience. For sure, Charlie wanted to talk to Hermit Chan before dusk, but he would take a moment to watch PL explore and appreciate the world around him.

Charlie thought part of PL's trademark eagerness was the twinkling in his eyes—a slight smile on his face. He'd seen them both before, many times, and with several degrees of enthusiasm. It would take two hands at least to count the times he ended up in a back corner of a bar—upscale and downscale—listening to PL go on about cameras, aerial photography, camera mounts, brands, and stabilizers. *Yep,* closing this film with an aerial fly-over was most probably in the cards for Pete.

Once again, Charlie reflected for a moment on PL's photographic brilliance.

And sometimes, times like these few moments, he wished he could share everything with PL. But he couldn't. Some secrets needed to stay compartmentalized.

* * * * *

Indeed, Pete Lily's interest in the Mojave, and this area around Rhodes Castle had continued to grow since his flyover only one short day ago. He felt captured by the quantity and magnitude of events since his stepping up and into that helicopter Saturday morning.

He hoped all the events since then, though quite exciting, wouldn't delay his second flight—then he caught himself. *Two men had died*—one awhile back, then lying rotting in a root cellar for who knows how long. And the other, Johnny Max—even though a man he'd met several times and didn't like, was possibly pushed off a balcony by his ex-wife—whom he had also met several times, and did like. And Hester said Leiv and Glover had been ambushed today?

More serious considerations than my taking more footage. He shook himself in a full-body shiver-type movement.

Pete wasn't really paying attention to where he was going—just getting a feel for the land. To that end, he was jigging-n-jagging around the terrain in front of Rhodes Castle for want of being able to move forward film-wise. Charlie was taking a pause for some reason. *The murders no doubt.* "Back to it later in the week," the movie-maker had promised.

But Pete needed to work—*well*, needed to *experience* was more to the truth. *It's just how I am.*

He felt a sharp sting in his calf, and looked down—then smiled as he pulled his jeans pants leg out of a small bush. He could not recall the name of the bush, though he did remember being told about it, and warned to look out by Hermit. Fortunately, he didn't fall directly into the ubiquitous desert plant, just brushed it enough to gather a few small land-mine shaped-thorns.

"Tenacious little devils, aren't you?" he said, while gingerly pulling them out of his pant leg. He was alone. No agreeing or contradicting voices. He did wonder at the strangeness of a place that harbored plants that caused him to smile while simultaneously doing him bodily harm.

His smile was also self-deprecating, in that while appreciative of his own tenacity, he recognized it as bordering on uncontrolled bull-doggedness. His camera hung from his shoulder, and he was looking for just the right spot to get an unusually-angled shot of the castle to his rear. The right vantage point was key—all important. *Just like with my flyover.*

Indeed, as with all his photography, he considered the effort to find the perfect vantage-point well worth a few leg stings from prickly desert thorns, contortionist maneuvers, and a few scrapes and bruises. Pete's smile broadened as his mind moved on to flying in the helicopter again to capture the closing fly-over frames for "Route 66 – Then and Now." He didn't know what music Marilyn would choose, that would come in the cutting room, probably during the first cut, he and Marilyn working with Charlie to put it all together. Though he knew Charlie would sneak a peek as soon as he could.

It was a thought which brought him back to photography, and an earlier interest when he first heard about Johnny Max. Getting shots at his funeral. Wherever and whenever that turned out to be. Ghoulish in a way, but JM was a heartthrob soap star—admittedly almost a has-been, but still, a name recognized by many. He would probably be buried in Hollywood style. Of course there would be a big memorial, televised with all the appropriate expressions of grief, accolades, and of course, designer funeral duds.

Pete stopped in his tracks as a realization hit him like lightning. *He didn't want* to film the funeral. *He didn't want* to film movie-people ever again. Scenery, aerial photography, fly-overs—that's what called him now. In an instant—Pete Lily's outlook toward life, and his career changed dramatically.

"Oh my," he said aloud.

Then Pete got one of those funny feelings like someone was watching him. He turned around quickly and looked back

133

toward Rhodes Castle. *No one.* Dusk was beginning to fall, but he was able to see Leiv's pickup pull out of the grandiose carriage house. For a moment he thought maybe Leiv had been watching him—but doubted it, not from that angle and over there. He did think it odd the man wasn't laid up in bed after what Hester said had happened.

"These desert people," he mumbled, not really knowing what he meant.

He shrugged and moved on, more toward the west and a direct view of the sunset. Pete then raised his Canon to eyelevel and started shooting. Maybe he could catch a reflection of the sunset as it played on the castle's facade. And maybe tomorrow, he could do the same with that wonderful chimney.

Ideas he couldn't stop flooded Pete's mind.

Before Leiv left Rhodes Castle to visit the second lady he needed to see this evening, and even though some pain was returning, he walked up and around back, finding his way to his and LC's special place. And once inside LC's cave, the familiar, remarkable, and much-cherished experience of connecting over time with LC Rhodes became a reality—and that *reality* soothed not only his heart, but also his body. The cave's impact was just a "brain" thing, his logical mind knew. *But still, sometimes....*

He still remembered the first time he "connected." So unexpected and unbelievable. Here in LC's hidden lair—just a small cavern really—but made into "something" special by LC. Even though—and quite unlike the library—the cavern had few accoutrements, it was surprisingly comfortable. And dry.

Most importantly, Leiv felt uncannily close to LC there. Especially when he stretched out in his grandfather's near fifty-year-old Eames chair and purposely closed his eyes even though it was close to pitch-black inside. There were a couple oil lamps from bygone days, but Leiv seldom lit them.

Even though dry, the air inside had a unique coolness, with the temperature moderate every time he visited. Leiv figured the cave's climate was somehow tied to its position, located on an uphill path around back of Rhodes Castle, with an angled and rather hidden entrance.

And the cave's smell was unique and quite easy on his sinuses. In fact, part of his stretching out and communicating ritual often included several deep breaths of "cave air." Oddly, LC never mentioned in his journal how he located his special cave, just that it was there.

This evening, his eyes closed, body relaxed and stretched out, Leiv waited. Waited for LC. His grandfather was deceased for almost thirty years now, and probably hadn't used his chair for forty to fifty years—yet for Leiv in moments like this, he was very much alive.

Present or not, this evening, Leiv asked LC his advice on how to approach Elizabeth-May. How to give her what he needed to give her. *Yes,* there was one more special lady he needed to settle matters with. *Elizabeth-May.*

It was unusual for sure, for Leiv to actually drive somewhere anytime near dusk or evening. But tonight it felt right. *And* he was compelled—his decision made firm somewhere between returning from LC's cave and grabbing a heavier jacket from the first floor hall closet. He moved quickly and rather stealthily. He didn't want to run into any movie-makers until later tonight.

The aroma of fresh bread permeated the inside air he rushed through. *Heavenly,* he thought. And as Leiv went through the kitchen heading toward his pickup, he stopped in his dash to move quickly, stooped down, and patted Dobie on the head. When he got up he was surprised to see HM staring at him. Then a once-in-a-lifetime occurrence happened. She smiled at him—

and he smiled back.

Nonetheless, within seconds, and as if nothing unusual had transpired, Hester asked for confirmation, "Everyone will be here tonight?"

Leiv nodded, and thought he detected a lilt to her voice, but quickly dashed the thought as ridiculous. He was making too much out of one little smile.

"And *all* them film crew will still be here?"

He nodded again, wondered in passing why she was so particular about them *all* being present, then proceeded to take the few steps to the garage's kitchen door entrance. As he closed the door behind him, Leiv saw David Milhouse stick his head in the kitchen door and ask, "Is now an okay time to talk? What with everything you have to do?"

Leiv wanted to eavesdrop, but made himself behave and closed the door. Yet, his curiosity played out several ridiculous HM and David scenarios while getting in his little truck, and then while driving down the castle's circular driveway.

But once Leiv reached the main paved road and headed toward Elizabeth-May's—dusk in Shiné caught hold of his senses, heart, and emotions. From LC's cave, it was clearly dusk and its accompanying sunset weren't far away in time; but now, not much later, and with the addition of a broader and more panoramic-like view of the western horizon, he was taken aback. So much so, at the risk of nightfall encompassing him—Leiv pulled onto the shoulder and got out of his car to take in the sunset for a couple moments.

Gorgeous, he thought. From red to the palest of yellows, and from saturated sweeping brushstrokes of color to wispy streaks of accent—to his eye, there was no comparison anywhere he'd so far lived. *What a surprise.*

Then things changed a bit. For some reason he took a couple steps forward and the same type of unexpected Mojave whirlwind that had taken "the book" away hit him face on. The odd part was, the gust felt wonderful. The wind's force was enough for him to expect to be buffeted at a minimum, pushed around a bit. Accompanied by a gentle nudge at the most. *But no, it was more like a refreshing wash across his skin.* His whole body even felt refreshed, though clothed and bundled up in a jeans-jacket to protect against the invariable nighttime chill. It was a most unusual circumstance and Leiv said aloud, "I wish Melissa were here to experience this with me."

And for the first time since he'd come back to Shiné, Leigh-Everett Rhodes realized he wouldn't be here in the Mojave *if* Melissa were still alive. *If* together, they would be experiencing a completely different life path. *What-ifs were powerful stuff.*

The emotion those thoughts brought—standing alone, at dusk in the middle of Mojave with miles of open desert before him—were overwhelmingly confusing. He stood there, an all-encompassing dust devil swirl passing over and around him—unable to move for several long, long minutes.

After Charlie pulled himself away from watching PL, and after he was sure Leiv was well on his way to wherever, he headed out himself—commandeering their film van for his personal use. He left via Rhodes Castle's front door to avoid running into Hester or any of his team members. Once on the actual road, he didn't look down the road leading to Elizabeth-May's, where he intuited Leiv Rhodes might be heading.

Of course his mind *was* on Chan. He wanted to talk to him one more time before moving on. Charlie was drawn to the man, but unable to put his finger on why that was. For sure, he was struck with the man's intelligent-looking and inquisitive eyes. He just didn't fit any "desert-rat" caricature he had so far formulated. In fact, Charlie even liked the sound of Douglas "Hermit" Chan's whole name, and used it when calling him earlier to make arrangements for a second visit.

This time I'll have my one-on-one talk.

*   *   *   *   *

Invite secured, and the short drive accomplished, Charlie was now sitting at half-angles to Douglas "Hermit" Chan in a matching and surprisingly comfortable rough-hewn log chair. Well padded of course, and *not unattractive*. Between them was a medium-sized table, again log-hewn, but with a dark maroon-patterned tabletop. They were in a nook off the kitchen, with a floor to ceiling glass view to the west. Charlie felt quite comfortable.

Funny, how I never noticed furnishings until I did that series. He called his new appreciation for furnishings a "takeaway." He left every shoot with at least one or two such insights. After a little time and distance had passed, he wondered what would he'd take away from "Route 66—Then and Now?" *Maybe these moments here with Douglas?*

Both men were sipping from snifters—his, B&B liqueur, Hermit's, Gentleman Jack whiskey. And they were alone in his upscale log home—if you didn't count the cats—just the situation Charlie had hoped for. Not like the first time when his whole crew descended upon the man. *Jeez, only a day ago.*

"This is nice." Charlie spoke his thoughts to Hermit, a hoard of benevolently encircling cats, and the world in general.

"Yeah," Douglas agreed softly—evidently caught up in Charlie's moments of appreciation.

"Do you remember yesterday when we first came to your house? And you served us whiskey at eight in the morning?" Charlie still couldn't get over the early-morning booze aspect of their first visit. A visit when he initially thought he wanted to talk to this man again. Alone. *Now here we are.*

Hermit laughed. "Maybe I should have made tea that morning?"

"Which reminds me," Charlie half mused, half asked, "do you use a cell phone?"

"Of course. Doesn't everyone?"

"Where are the cell towers? Closest I've seen are along the highways."

Douglas laughed, and Charlie thought it might be at him, but preferred to think it was "with him," as the hackneyed saying went.

"Look like trees. Fake branches. You've seen 'em, just don't know you have."

"And we all missed them." *Including PL with his sharp eye.* "You knew then, yesterday morning, about that chimney, didn't you?" Charlie recognized he had switched topics and jumped right into another one of his curiosities about this man without segue-type words.

Hermit emptied his snifter of Gentleman Jack in one walloping swallow, set it on the table next to two still half-full cut-crystal decanters and asked, "You want another?"

Charlie shook his head. "Not yet." He needed to keep a halfway clear head. *Leiv Rhodes will probably be serving booze too.*

"Well," Hermit returned to his question with what Charlie took as a genuinely thoughtful look. "I don't know what you mean by 'knew.'"

Charlie laughed. "Well for starters, 'knew' Elizabeth-May's place was only a few miles down the road. And 'knew' that's where the chimney stood that Pete was talking about."

Hermit made a face and a bemused clicking sound out the corner of his mouth. "Well, I guess you got me there."

An all black cat—except for a white circle around its nostrils, and another covering about two-inches on the end of its tail—jumped in Hermit's lap. Before Charlie had completely taken in his host's cat-invader, a calico jumped in his own lap. Until told otherwise, Charlie thought of cats as female, and dogs as male. *Something psychological there.* Then without thought he started stroking the calico in his lap, and cooed in a childlike tone he didn't know he was capable of, "There, there, pretty girl." Not knowing what to make of his own inexplicable actions and

139

words, Charlie looked over at Hermit who was doing the same thing. Stroking and cooing.

"It's addictive." Hermit Chan could evidently also read minds.

"I...I—"

"They're in control. Just surrender."

Charlie did as bid. "Why didn't you want to tell us about the chimney?"

"I don't know." Hermit gestured with his head toward his empty snifter. "Sure you don't want another one?"

Charlie looked again at his almost empty snifter, then placed it on the side table next to Douglas's and smiled. "If you insist." *Can't help it.* Clearly too much B&B already, *and I'm about to have more.* "But only a third—I still have to drive tonight."

Charlie watched as Douglas half-refilled both their snifters. Outside evening was sneaking up on them, with the sky turning an orange red—with distinct slashes across the horizon—but clearly with intent to blend in one vibrant hue. Actually, the horizon seemed more like a brush stroke painting. Some lines of color firm and broad, others barely wisps of color. He sure hoped PL could see the picture he was witnessing from Rhodes Castle. *Maybe taking pictures?*

Along with the beauty he was witnessing outside, Charlie's senses also took in the distinct aroma of the B&B Hermit had just poured—while simultaneously feeling the warmth spreading through his body from what he'd already consumed.

"The aroma off the side of the glass while pouring is the best," Hermit remarked—making it crystal clear he was able to slide in and out of Charlie's thoughts at will. He added, "A few clouds coming in from Arizona I expect. That's why the colors are so bright and so early." He paused in thought for a moment. "Or maybe coming in from the west. Something I'd usually sense." He tilted his head a bit before fading off into thought.

Another set of Charlie's senses pulled him up short—reminding him he needed to be on guard. There were areas of his brain he could not let Hermit intuit—liking the man notwithstanding.

He asked, "You like Elizabeth-May, don't you?" Charlie was heading down another path without a clue why he wanted to pursue the point with Douglas, and consequently jumped right in without forethought. *None of my business.* Yet when he saw the chagrined look on Hermit's face, he knew his comment was on the mark—making him feel even more ashamed he'd asked.

Then Hermit looked down at his blue jean-clad knees for a second. "I guess I am a bit smitten."

"Smitten," Charlie repeated with admiration. "A word my grandmother used." *What a charming man.* At that moment, Charlie realized he had picked up an addition to what he called his "friends for life" list. It was a short list.

"Got the phrase from Everett Rhodes, who said he got it from his father LC."

"The man who started this town?"

"You got it." Then Hermit proceeded at a leisurely pace to tell Charlie about the history, as he was told, about Shiné.

Pleasant time, all in all, Charlie thought yet again after hearing what he considered a most remarkable tale of a most remarkable man. When Douglas finished, Charlie asked, "Do you think The Mojave-Stone really exists?"

"Of course it does. Just don't know where the wily-old-geezer hid it."

The look in David's eye when he met Hester Miller, flashed back to Charlie in vivid detail. Along with the story his set designer shared with the team about LC's supposed "Cooper" lineage. "What about the Romani claim to the stone?"

"Silly nonsense."

A comfortable and lengthy pause fell between the two men and purring cats—two in their laps, and the gang previously milling about having settled into positions at their feet, or in furniture leg niches. All purring it seemed to him—like background music to a shoot. And Charlie making sure he didn't drink anymore booze before driving back to the castle.

Hermit broke their silence. "Did I mention I was a fireman before I settled out here?"

Surprised again, Charlie said, "Ah—no, you didn't." Hermit certainly didn't look like a fireman. He asked, "Where?"

"Chicago."

Charlie waited. He had a feeling Douglas was about to tell him something special. Something rather personal. Oddly, he felt honored, and accordingly waited patiently.

"There was this warehouse fire once. At night. It was a big warehouse. A big fire. Lots of flames, smoke, and drafts. All chasing us instead of us chasing them. Sometimes it's like that." Hermit's gaze moved from Charlie to the sunset outside his log cabin's picture window. As he listened, Charlie's attention was also drawn outside.

Eerie and quite nice. The brilliant slashes of red and regular old orange had morphed into a brilliant orange glow that seemed to fill the entire horizon. Now an orange the color of fire. *Not really,* he pushed his fanciful vision back. But he knew his eyes were seeing a sunset painted really close to the color of fire flames. "What an orange," he mumbled aloud.

Douglas didn't seem to hear him and went on with his story. "It was five of us."

A quick look back at Hermit's face told Charlie his new friend was also captured by the symbolic sunset even though he hadn't said anything. "We got turned around," Hermit continued. "All of us. Didn't happen that often that we all got disoriented. But it did that night."

Charlie took a deep breath. Scared of what Douglas might be telling him next.

"Then this little boy came running up to me, yelling at all of us actually—and his words were clear as a bell. 'Follow me, follow me. This is the way out.' We did follow him, up all the way to the roof by a back staircase we would never have found. We eventually got up on the roof and the Ladder Company got us down." He took a moment before finishing. "The boy disappeared into thin air. We never found a boy, alive or dead. And believe me we searched. He led us out, then he was gone."

"Disappeared?"

"Or didn't exist." Douglas lifted his snifter and drained the last sips. Then a slow smile spread across his face.

"A ghost," Charlie whispered, and realized he liked this man even more.

"Some say a ghost. My wife said a guardian angel."

Charlie took from Hermit's tone his wife was deceased. Didn't need to ask. But once again to his great surprise, an almost overwhelming wish rose from somewhere that his new friend would one day soon—*well, spoon was probably the appropriate word to go with smitten*—with one widow named Elizabeth-May Logan. He almost laughed at what his non-movie business compatriots would think of that word. "Smitten" most definitely would not be in their vocabulary. And never before had he wanted to play cupid.

Charlie smiled, and his artistic self fancied that he—The Movie-Maker—was in a movie himself. *Hermit Chan's movie.*

And Hermit Chan's role in this movie? Charlie had initially seen him in a dramatic role when it came to his documentary and this Shiné adventure. Now he realized, belatedly and gratefully, Hermit's role was to become Charlie's new good friend. Not part of the main action—but as a friend he liked and admired— an important role indeed. Not many in his life had fit-the-bill.

They were standing side by side looking out her living room front window.

It was a striking and contrasting scene Leiv saw: the horizon's backdrop for the finishing sunset was the most unusual shade of orange—while close in, his vision and mind were forced to also take in crime-scene tape surrounding the burned out foundation of Elizabeth-May's grandparent's home. Root cellar and chimney included.

Between the two—crime-scene-wrapped foundation and vivid horizon—Mojave scrub desert seemed to alternately stand out, then recede into darkness at different spots stretching all the way to Shiné Ridge's horizon line.

Inside, where they stood, Elizabeth-May's sitting room was comfortingly warm, and smelled like flowers. Leiv guessed she used a spray scent. *Lilac?*

"Tempe is extremely smart, isn't he?" Leiv said as he looked down at the German Shepherd standing between them— who was in-kind looking up at him with an intense canine gaze. Then quite unexpectedly, given the protective instincts Leiv imagined were at play with Tempe's positioning of himself, the intelligence he attributed to the Shepherd, and the look he saw in the canine's eyes—Leiv thought Tempe winked at him.

Poor silliness. But silly or not about the actual wink, a piece of Leiv's psyche identified something in Tempe's eyes and stance that confirmed what Leiv was sure happened a few years back.

"Tony was my soul mate." Elizabeth-May turned her gaze from the horizon, and for a moment her eyes met his, intent and direct, yet still soft as befitting the era her dress and earrings evoked—and her voice beseeching. "Do you know what it means to have a soul mate? Know what it feels like?" Seemingly from out of nowhere, she brought a white handkerchief laced with embroidery, to the corner of her right eye.

She caught Leiv unawares, and before he could pull his emotions back, he had to swallow hard to ward off a lump rising in his throat. *Melissa, my love.* In the process of taking back control of his emotions, he barely managed an acknowledging nod.

After a nod of her own, Elizabeth-May next said, "I can see from your eyes you have. You know the feeling here." She touched her heart, and he could see her nails were painted pink.

The style maybe a generation ago? Maybe two, he mused without intent, purpose, or direct knowledge. *A young woman,* he thought, *wanting to make sure her femininity was known.*

"When Tony died my world changed forever." She turned back to what was now becoming the dregs of the sunset. "You know my grandparents were one of the first families to build here after LC announced he was 'starting a town.'" Elizabeth-May laughed lightly. "It was a different kind of time."

"I know." If she only knew about all the details he'd read in his grandfather's diary, all the ins and outs of Shiné's development, all LC's secrets from way back when. As it turned out, her grandfather, Jules, was his grandmother Violet's brother. According to LC, Jules was not only a friend, but also extended family.

He next said, "I wanted to see how you were doing." With his words, the connection came to Leiv for the first time. Elizabeth-May and he were cousins.

"I'm actually doing well."

He turned his head slightly to look at her, and saw she was smiling.

"Feeling pretty lucky, actually," she said.

Leiv was surprised. Not the response he expected.

"Would you like some tea?" Her offer and voice were inviting.

But he needed to get back soon. "I'm not staying long." He let a moment pass, then asked, "Why are you feeling lucky?"

"I've been expecting Glover, or Glover and higher-ups to descend on me. Arrest me for killing that man in the root cellar, and for marrying and harboring a known gangster." She reached out, touched the window, then returned her hand to her side.

Leiv did the same. The glass was warm. *As it should be,* he thought.

Yet Elizabeth-May said, "Cool, right?"

He could feel Tempe watching his every move. "I don't think there's much cause to worry about being arrested." Then he waited. Waited for Elizabeth-May, as he was sure she would, to understand via their moment of silence, that he knew the truth. But also, and most importantly, that he would never say anything about their joint crime. Tempe was a very smart dog, indeed.

Next Leiv slipped his right hand into his pants pocket and rubbed his fingers over the polished rock he picked up at Elizabeth's chimney remains. It was smooth and lovely to his touch. Then he removed the precious stone from his pocket, and crossing his arm over Tempe, slipped it into her hand.

In Leiv's mind, in that instant—LC, Viola, and Elizabeth-May's destinies came full circle.

"What is this?" she asked, in a tone that sounded to Leiv's ear like she already knew.

"Your grandfather's Mojave-Stone." Inside he smiled. A smile he fancied crossed back across two generations.

When he exited the van, David was waiting for Charlie outside the front door of Rhodes Castle. Then with a nod, but no words, both headed side-by-side walking down the circular driveway toward the main road.

"Pete and Marilyn were waiting for you so they can pack everything up," David said.

"Not that much I wouldn't think," Charlie said. "Mainly shower stuff for me." He looked down at his jeans. "And I just dragged in one change of clothes." He smiled inwardly. Davey was not only a breeze to work with, but also interesting, intelligent, and a logistic whiz. And with an ability to be quite duplicitous as was required. The only negative he could say about Davey was his Chicago relatives stunk, to put it mildly. Criminals who liked being criminals and not looking for a different way. Old ways were still good ways to them. Fortunately, Davey thought the same about his relatives. Hence, his presence on Charlie's non-movie-making team.

Changing the subject, Charlie informed Davey, "I cut out the one frame that caught Nightshade in the bushes. PL would have seen him for sure and asked about it. I thought he was out there." *I could feel him.* Charlie pre-screened all film before the official "Director's Cut." He was known for it by PL, and industry wide. No one ever second-guessed his presence scrutinizing frames at whatever synchronizer they were using— in studio or portable like here.

"You were in the van early this morning while we were still sleeping?" David smiled.

Charlie nodded.

"Glad you got a frame at least." David released a small disparaging sigh. "Last update I got from the LA lab was they were having a hard time pinpointing his location when I talked to him on the phone that one time. He said something about Shiné Ridge had some good hiding-out spots."

"It was Nightshade, right?" Charlie clicked his teeth reminiscent of Glover. "You're sure."

"Oh yeah, I'd know that voice, even when the reception is so horrible. He was trying to get info out of me. I played dumb of course."

"Of course." Charlie smiled. "That's why the confusion about Lookout Loop and Shiné Ridge when we were heading up to Chan's? You didn't want PL getting in the middle of something."

Davey nodded. "Now, on the blood sample from the body in the root celler. It's Alex, they're pretty sure. More fancy tests being done, but you know all that usually takes ages—but there's heavyweight pressure from pretty high up. And evidently there's a rather efficient lab in Vegas. Latest equipment." They both smiled at the same time. "And high-up connections. A whole team has been assigned to Nightshade. Not our problem anymore. We're off assignment on this one. They think he's on his way to Florida was the one tidbit they threw my way. I think they're probably right."

"Does Alex have a last name that you know of?"

David shook his head.

"And the journal?" Charlie asked. One of the many things that annoyed him about the FBI was the compartmentalization. Then there was the lack of departmental communication. *They'd never be able to do what I do. Be a movie-maker like me.* Charlie smiled at his own silly comparison between the organizational communication and fraternization required of a film producer versus the FBI.

"Wall of silence." Davey took a hefty, long, and appreciative-sounding deep breath. As if he actually liked the desert air. "Wouldn't surprise me if we've got agents out scouring the desert looking for sheets of paper."

"It's a big desert." Charlie chuckled. "But Jack is scheduled to go on another flyover with PL. Maybe tomorrow."

"Does PL know anything about Jack?"

"Not as far as I know."

David stopped walking, causing Charlie to also stop. Then he looked in back of them and to both sides. "Just us right now." He lowered his voice a tad. "Would you go back to the East Coast if they called you in?"

"No." He was first and foremost a film maker. *The FBI can go to hell if I have to make a choice.* "While we're getting personal, what's with you and this Miller woman?"

David chuckled lightly. "Not my type right?"

Charlie made a quizzical face. "Vice versa. And would you go back to Chicago if they asked you?" He hoped his countenance didn't display how incompatible Hester Miller and David Milhouse seemed to him on so many levels. She was rather short, he was tall: she was dowdy and matronly in body language and dress, while he was stylish: she had a dour, bordering on sour resident expression, while David's normal countenance spoke of a smile in the making. And as snooty, elitist, and outright biased as he knew his comparison was—she was a housekeeper and he was an accomplished set-designer. *My mother's first job was as a housekeeper.* This remembrance of his mother caught Charlie up short—*I need to come down off my high horse.* And as if to emphasize how wrong-thinking his analysis was, he watched as a wistful expression Charlie had never seen before crossed his set designer and fellow FBI undercover agent's face.

Then in a tone dripping in the incomprehensible wistfulness of the newly smitten, David said in response to Charlie thoughts, "I'm in love."

Charlie waited.

After a moment, David continued, "There is *no* explanation, Charlie. *No* alternate objective. *No* long-term plan—*no* explanation I can think of—let alone understand or rationalize." He repeated his declaration. "I'm in love."

Charlie didn't know what to say, but fortunately felt his cell phone vibrate in his pants pocket. He took it out and looked at the number. "Not now," he said with a sigh. He looked over to David who was also looking at the face of his cell phone.

"No, not now," he echoed Charlie.

Then the two men stared at each other for a long moment. Charlie broke their silent communication. "I can see a TV pilot, 'Reluctant G-Men.'"

"Or 'FBI Agents. Behind the Camera.'"

"Or—" Charlie couldn't think of another one, but began laughing and couldn't immediately stop when David joined in.

"No one would believe you're an agent," David said when he could talk seriously again.

"And you think you look like a G-man?" In fact, Charlie knew they were so similar in "type," he and David had been confused for each other in the past. On several occasions.

They started laughing again. Eventually David was able to say with a straight face, "I'm going to the van to grab a scarf I bought for Hester earlier today."

Charlie wanted to laugh again, but forced himself to smile pleasantly and nod his head. "I think she'll like it." Actually, from what he glimpsed in the van earlier going to Hermit's—Charlie had wondered who or what the scarf was for. He couldn't imagine who would like it—to him, it was pretty darned ugly. Well, more like gaudy. Several shades of bright red, yellow, and light blues. *Oh yeah, and luminescent green edged in purple if he was remembering correctly.*

Then he remembered an important item—David's newly-beloved claimed Romani heritage. And with a change of mind, heart, and perspective—Charlie realized what a great selection David had made, given what he'd seen of her taste, and what he figured was important to her. *Must have paid a fortune to have it delivered so quickly, and out here in Mojave-land*—but he didn't remember seeing a delivery truck? "Where did you get it?" he asked.

His set designer smiled broadly. "Found it on a back shelf at Shiné Pump and Fill. Right next door to TGS. On a shelf next to a Route 66 beer stein."

Charlie exchanged a "go-figure" gesture with David, and reflected for a moment over his sense of wonderment. This desert was definitely not his cup-of-tea—but on this shoot he'd met Hermit Douglas—a new friend for life. And with his crew's help, he was filming what he figured was going to be the best travel documentary ever done. He was already lining up in his mind the film awards and festivals "Route 66 - Then and Now" would garner. And a follow-on TV special maybe.

And David is in love with the most unlikely person I could possibly imagine. "Yep, the hell with the FBI," he said softly, and intended for his own ears. *I've changed.* Here in this god-forsaken desert, and pretty much out-of-the-blue, he'd ended up "living" some special moments. *And from the inside, looking out.* Up to this point in his life, Charlie realized he'd been looking in, filmmaking and FBI wise. Not a bad thing—actually the reason why he was such a good producer. But *living* life, too, was also important.

This time, re-thinking about the smitten pair, he not only tapped his forehead with three fingers, but also made a clicking sound out the corner of his mouth. Charlie realized he stole this new mannerism from Shiné's Chief of Police, Glover Deers—and evidently internalized.

His cell phone rang again. "Jack," the caller ID informed him.

This call he decided to take. Jack was not only an FBI agent, but also an experienced helicopter pilot—recruited just for this assignment.

Charlie asked, "Yeah, Jack, what do you have for me?" Charlie listened, then said, "Great you've re-scheduled with PL. I'll be interested if you see anything enlightening when you go up." Enlightening was their own private G-man-code-word.

Glover unpinned the picture-poster of Alex-*no last name* from his break-area corkboard, walked over, then slipped it into the folder-basket on his desk. Vegas had relayed the info to DC, they had relayed the info to Chicago, who had relayed the ID info back to Vegas with instructions, who had in turn relayed the info to Needles, and Deputy Brad Temper had relayed the info to him. *All in one day.* Evidently the Feds, Chicago cops, Vegas cops, and three agencies put a hell of a lot of pressure on somebody's forensics lab. Glover didn't know which lab, but he'd never seen results come back this fast. *Unheard of actually, except on TV.* And there it all was, in an electronically-sent and now printed report. He had heard something about a new rapid DNA system. *Maybe in Vegas?* Regardless, he was glad for the information.

Alex had somehow found his way into Elizabeth-May's root cellar. *Good place for him by my way of thinking.* Not a kind thought, but he didn't care. He certainly wasn't about to instigate any charges against Elizabeth-May. And no agency was asking him to.

Now, he needed to head home. A shower and change of clothes were on the agenda. He started his "closure procedure,"

151

activating all the necessary switches and messages that directed after-hours callers to the State Police, or 911. *Coffee pot off. Cooling room light off.*

He hadn't taken anymore of Walker's pain pills—didn't much care about how they made him feel. Consequently, Glover now ached all over. It was a price he would have to pay. Tonight was an extra "withdrawing-room" night at Leiv's, and he wasn't about to miss it. An event he'd come to enjoy over the last few months. He especially liked checking up on his mother without it being obvious. Just a mother and son sharing an evening at a friend's place sort-of-thing. And tonight was special. Sort of a goodbye to the film crew. He didn't have a reason to hold or question them further, and no other jurisdiction had asked him to do that either. The lack of interest in the film crew by other jurisdictions was a little odd—he didn't care.

I know Elizabeth-May somehow got Alex in the root cellar and locked him in. But there was no evidence, and he didn't think there was anything he could do to get any evidence. And the most important part—once again, he didn't care. A realization Glover planned to think on a bit. Not an admirable perspective in a law and order professional. This moment, however, he didn't give a damn.

Besides, with a Chicago "hit man" now being bandied about, there wouldn't be any pressure on Elizabeth-May or Mary Jones. Glover allowed himself a little smile there. He also figured Mary Jones had given Johnny Max a little shove. But now—enter the hit man as the likeliest suspect. *Damnedest thing that.*

Glover was also frank enough with himself to realize he wanted the social time at Leiv's. Especially tonight. He needed to get rid of the funk that wouldn't go away over losing that book. Watching it blow away toward the dunes. *Awful.* It was a mental misery worse than anything he was physically feeling.

He would go into Needles tomorrow, do a lot of explaining. Not that he didn't do his part toward the investigation over the last day. Even had Pete Lily print up a pile of digital pictures for him from the root cellar scene.

With keys in hand, he headed toward the front door. He didn't usually like unsolved cases, loose ends. But he didn't mind this time. *Except for....* Glover stopped, smiled, turned back, and went to his desk. *Some loose ends take generations to come together.* But eventually they're solved. Once at his desk, he bent over and unlocked the thin top drawer he kept special evidence in. As expected, they were still there. Both of them.

Two rough pebbles, polished by him last night, now smooth and rather pretty opals. Rocks he picked up at Elizabeth-May's in front of her chimney, after he'd seen Leiv "palm" something from the ground. *Leiv's a sly one alright.* Glover wasn't exactly sure why these two in the same area caught his eye, but they did. A flash? A twinkle? An otherworldly calling? Or just plain blind luck. Leiv had seen one, he'd seen two more.

The items he had in his drawer were something special. That he knew. Glover also knew he and Leiv would have to have a conversation down the road about the Mojave-Stones.

Chapter Five

Smitten – Past and Present

*From LC's journal: One thing I can say about this here town I've
created. Shiné. It's quiet. Nothing ever happens. Just the way I like it.
Just the way Viola likes it. Good place to raise our kids. It's that way
because we know it ain't about what them law books say. It's just about
doing what's right.*

*From LC's journal: Gall dang it, do I love sitting around on Saturday
nights gabbing with my friends. A fire cracking, one of my stones
staring back at me. Viola did this for me. Made this room special. I'll
never forget her kindness. Never. No wonder I'm so smitten with that
woman.*

Leiv could restate another passage verbatim *from LC's journal:*
*They got the saying all wrong by my way of thinking. Where ya sit ain't
necessarily where ya stand. Like me, sat with the Coopers most of my
youth. But I've stood and still stand as a Rhodes for most of my life
now. Started the Mojave-Stove thing myself, but claimed there ain't one
from where I've sat all these years here in Shiné. Standing, I know
there's five stone. that's wrong—eight if I count the ones in Jules's*

155

chimney. *All of em, right out there in plain sight. Ha! to 'em all. Except for my love Viola...and now my little grandson Leigh-Everett. They are my heart.*

Still Sunday...

"I'm too old for changes like this," Hester told Dobie who was asleep under her kitchen worktable.

For sure, she had never felt anything like this in her whole life. Consequently, and so unlike the Hester Miller she thought she was, she sat at her kitchen table doing nothing for a long time after David left. Even though her mother had always cautioned against idle hands.

But here she was, confronted with new-world possibilities. *What to think, what to do?* She was a gypsy—in name, heart, and soul—at least that's how she'd thought of herself for all her life. She was Hester Miller Senior's daughter, which meant she was also crusty, and occasionally vindictive.

Could she be a different person? Her upbringing, her genetic makeup, the way she looked at the world weren't anything like this Milhouse guy. *A LA hotshot scene designer. Or did he say set designer?* And what the heck was the difference, anyway?

But it was his wanting to go to Chicago first, talk to Bersch with her. Find out where Nadya had disappeared to. Meet his family. *Too fast*, Hester thought. Hard for her to absorb all his ideas and plans. And then they'd come back to Los Angeles. *LA.* Her mother had called it movie-land.

"Ha," she said aloud. *And they'd drive there on Route 66, and take Dobie with them.* That wasn't her? Was it? Then Hester remembered a story her mother had told her about the early days, about gypsies coming across the country. *Heck, LC was actually a Cooper.* And he traveled The Route to get here. *In tougher days than this.* David said they would rent a camper.

She let herself dream for a moment about alien actions,

alien worlds outside Rhodes Castle. Then once again she caught herself, reminded herself—Chicago was not alien territory.

No, it was her perspective on the world that had changed—and was now changing again. Neither Chicago or Rhodes Castle would be the center of her universe. Neither would memories of LC, Everett—or even her mother Hester that would be her focus. Her universe would be David Milhouse. Hester could barely imagine that scenario. But he had made it seem so real, so doable. He'd made her believe.

She even showed him her room. He loved it, the colors, the rows, the drapes. Said they would make a great team designing sets together. *I just can't imagine.*

Of course she might have to dress different if she left Shiné. Though he hadn't said so. He seemed to like her as she was.

Hester brought her hand to her mouth. Then another thought attempted to hold back her fly-away dream. *Clueless Leigh-Everett.* He'd be alone.

But then, with insight rather new to her, and with the clarity of objective-thought Hester knew didn't often come her way—she understood. Leigh-Everett's talk with her earlier was intended to set her free. He would be fine. And since the Mojave-Stone did not exist, she consequently shouldn't care.

Mugs had heard a lot about Southern California drivers, so the only part of his escape he thought would be "iffy," turned out not that bad at all. He was traveling west *after* rush-hour, and for sure he had to keep his wits about him. The drivers left on the road were pushing it, but they seemed fairly skillful. The only sticky part was early on, a curvy downhill patch through something called Cajon Pass. The rest was just crappy expressway traffic. *Actually they call it a freeway,* he mused during his myriad of driving thoughts.

On purpose, Mugs arrived early for his evening flight, and when he saw it was between boarding times as hoped for, he found himself a perfect spot to sit in Terminal C, at gate 21 boarding area in John Wayne International Airport, Santa Ana. Indeed, there was a perfect seat waiting for him, in back, on the side, near the walkway, and with a clear view of foot traffic. He'd known night flights were the best. *Sometimes I'm just a damn lucky guy.*

Overall, he thought John Wayne a spacious airport, easy for him to keep an eye out for security or cops milling around; or worse, sizing him up. Not that he was carrying—and he was dressed in casual business clothes. *Just another weary corporate schmuck heading home.*

He figured they would be staking out McCarran, maybe Ontario, possibly LAX, but not John Wayne. True enough, he also considered Long Beach, but ultimately selected John Wayne because he liked the sound of Santa Ana. "Hah." He complemented his bright thinking under his breath, even though there was no one in hearing range; *but I'm a professional. Always careful.* And the cops didn't give up. He figured they were still looking for his predecessor Alex. *But seems like he's disappeared from the face of the earth?* Though he doubted that podunk Shiné police department had a brain to split between them, much less any of the latest electronic gear to know what's going on in the rest of the world. Probably didn't even know he'd been around.

Besides, he hadn't really done anything, now had he? He finally found out in the Victorville newspaper he picked up during a pit-stop on the way to the airport, that Johnny Max had a stupid accident trying to woo back that soap opera star ex-wife of his. *Falling off a balcony of all things.* And he watched Anthony L's "insurance policy" fly-the-coop so to speak right before taking those Keystone Cops on the chase of their dull cop lives. He smiled slightly at his little flyaway witticism. *Maybe the only good thing about that damn desert. The winds.*

One regret was he didn't actually take-them-out. Thinking

they could catch him. Bring down Mugs Nightshade. *Ha!* On the other hand, if he'd killed a couple cops, even out there in the desert, there would probably be an all out manhunt for him right now.

His cousin's son, David Milhouse, a fancy LA set designer of all things, at his request, had supposedly driven to the ledge himself to see if there were any readable-hunks of book lying around. Reception had been awful. He still wasn't sure if David had orchestrated that little book-finding maneuver or not—but the kid was family, and as family, he could trust him. *Can't I?* And if he said the book was gone in all directions, it was.

Yep, all their secrets were safe. Davey had also mentioned on their one telephone conversation about a body in that root cellar hole. The cell phone reception had been horrible—*damn desert*—so Mugs didn't get any more details on that, because he was also taking the opportunity to get away from that place as that station wagon was arriving. Who knows how many years that body had been there? Not a concern of his.

With those thoughts, Mugs allowed himself a moment of relaxation, and closed his eyes. But true to character, instead of moving on to his getaway details, he thought some more about the completion of this job, and most importantly, his reputation. Again, he mentally reasserted the known fact Johnny Max was dead, *stroke of luck there.* And the pages of Anthony L's insurance policy book had become litter to be swallowed up in that damn-awful desert. Both circumstances were "fixed." Another job done. Though definitely not as he expected. But *yes,* he could relax knowing his reputation was intact. One more fix in Florida, and he would be back home, no one the wiser, and driving himself down to Vito's for calzone in his pearl-blue Acura.

Then Mugs shivered slightly at the thought of his last couple days in the Mojave. Definitely not his "cup of tea," as Lucky Francis was fond of saying. Evidently Lucky's son, Doc Francis liked the desert. *Go figure.*

"Not me, Chicago boy, born and bred." *No matter how*

much the city has changed. Mugs had surprised himself speaking aloud, and opened his eyes. He needed to pay attention, a flight crew and passengers could appear out of nowhere for boarding to Miami any time now. *I've changed, too*. He didn't know how or why, figuring that kind of stuff was not his bag. But changed he had. *Well, time will tell*. Maybe it was just he appreciated "his" city much more now that he'd seen this awful desert place. Involuntarily, Mugs shivered while blowing metaphorically distasteful puffs of air out both sides of his mouth.

He moved his mind forward to his next task at hand. *Yep*, he needed to start thinking about the quickie situation he needed to "fix" before finally heading back home. The call had come last night. Hopefully it wouldn't be too hot and muggy in Florida yet. Again, weather not up his alley. But he was a professional, now wasn't he?

Still, he allowed himself a moment or two of wistful memories, back on Paulina Street, playing "You're It" in his grandmother's backyard—mindful of course, not to go clomping around in the nightshade running along her alley fence. "Poisonous," she'd warned him many-a-time.

They easily, and quite naturally it seemed, took the same seats as the previous night. This evening though, would be a goodbye of sorts. *Two days only*, Leiv thought, *and so much has happened*.

"Nice," said Pastor Lloyd Apply sitting next to him, and sniffing the air with an uncharacteristic dramatic flair.

Leiv figured Shiné's pastor was referring to—*well, to everything*—he hoped. It was a pleasing assumption he wanted to think was truth.

"Love that fireplace," Pete Lily said from across the room. "Bet I could almost stand in it."

Still thinking about Lloyd's statement, Leiv did note a hint of eucalyptus floating on the air in LC's withdrawing-room. Sometimes Leiv found the scent overpowering. Not tonight. *Perfect.*

He would have to complement Hester on her fireplace wood mix. He lugged it all in from the garage, but she assembled the mix. To him, wood was wood. True enough, LC had gone on and on in one section of his journal on the virtues of various woods. A few names Leiv was familiar with and still remembered were eucalyptus, spruce, alder, and pine—but several others, apricot, almond, and walnut, had surprised him. Leiv searched for and found Internet pictures, but most of the trees he hadn't seen anywhere around Shiné.

Local habitat though, doesn't make much difference here at the castle, since HM ordered the stuff by the truckload from a place near Cajon Pass. The tree species might be unrecognizable to him, but Leiv did know for certain, the cords cost a fortune when you threw in the delivery. Nonetheless, and cost be damned, LC's monstrous fireplace gave him and others—as in Pete's remark—so much pleasure.

Even this time of year on these cool spring evenings, a fire was not only pleasing, but quite appropriate. Leiv took a moment to focus on tonight's modest fire in particular, crackling ever so slightly—then found himself smiling. *What would a withdrawing room be without a fire going?*

Then further thinking about Pete's observation from his armchair across the room sitting right in front of the fireplace, Leiv figured he must have seen a lot in his photographic life, and his thoughts went on to wonder how it would be to view the world with Pete's lens-eye-view.

"This *is* nice," Lloyd said once more, and again with more emotion than Leiv was accustomed to hearing in his friend's speech. The Pastor next closed his eyes and let his head drop back into the cushiony top of his armchair at Leiv's left side.

Belatedly, Leiv also recognized the aroma of HM's freshly-baked yeast bread mini loaves, wine, Bristol Crème, B&B, fruit punch, and coffee wafting in the aromatic mix around LC's withdrawing-room. Also vying for sensory recognition were the culinary aromas from the chocolate bite-sized fudge-looking goodies Margaret brought. Then there was Doc's famed deviled eggs—Leiv loved the onion and pickle smell. He just hadn't taken the time to notice.

Lloyd probably doesn't even recognize the details of what he's smelling. But he likes it. And Leiv liked that his friend did. He smiled, and nodded in Lloyd's direction even though the pastor's eyes were momentarily closed.

Pete was evidently also continuing to take in and appreciate his surroundings. "This is a really comfy chair." He wiggled his butt around for emphasis.

"Glad you like it." As a gracious host, Leiv thought he should provide a little background to his guests. To that end, he spent a few sentences filling the photographer in on the provenances of the chairs in front of the fireplace—which included Marilyn's to Pete's left and Doc Walker's to his right. Leiv explained how the frames were original, purchased by his grandfather in the nineteen-forties. Subsequently in the sixties, his father Everett had the leather and cushion stuffing replaced. They were replicas, but good ones of Victorian spoon-back armchairs.

Pete smiled in response, and gave him a look Leiv couldn't quite decipher. "Amazing about your grandfather." Then Pete looked away as if in thought, and when he looked back, Leiv saw a twinkle in his eye. "An amazing man. Ever thought of doing a documentary? Talking about his influence on you, your father, even Illinois politics, versus..."

Leiv laughed. "Versus Shiné castledom?"

Pete leaned forward toward him, speaking louder, as if wanting to make sure these particular words carried across the room. "It *is* an interesting story."

For a moment, Leiv did actually wonder if LC would like being brought into today's electronic age. Then he shook his head. "Don't think so. But I'll let you know if the idea ever takes hold with me."

"All I can do is ask." Pete fell back into his armchair's caress, a rather glowing smile on his face Leiv thought was partly alcohol induced. "And by the way," Pete's smile grew as he asked, "that alfalfa field down the road, do you know who owns it?"

Leiv shook his head again. Truth was, he owned it, came with Rhodes Castle, and he leased it to a local grower. Information he preferred to keep to himself.

"I took some pictures yesterday, then more this morning. Walked down there. The blue of the flowers was still great, and there were even more of these...well, it seemed like thousands, but I'm guessing it wasn't that many...of small little butterflies flying and landing all through them." Pete seemed to be re-visualizing. "I took more pictures than I expected." His voice was wistful.

Leiv also kept his own counsel regarding the charming-looking butterflies, called by some, Alfalfa Caterpillars, and considered pests. *Depends upon the lens you're viewing the world through, I guess.*

From Leiv's left, Lloyd came back to life, leaned forward also, and asked Pete, "What happens next on your film?"

Leiv took the opportunity to drop out from their patchwork-like conversation and drift away into his own thoughts. *We're all here.* Except for set designer David Milhouse. He initially arrived with the others, but quickly asked Leiv if he would mind if he just popped into the kitchen to say hello to Hester Miller. "She said she made some special 'gypsy tea' for me."

Leiv had said yes of course, but remained dumbfounded by this unlikely attraction between HM and this sophisticated LA set designer. Which reminded him of something he wanted to ask Charlie. *What was the need for a set designer in the middle of the Mojave?* Didn't make sense to him.

Even though Leiv liked the fire, it was getting a little

warm for his taste. *Could be the Harvey's I've already consumed.* But some of the "heat" he knew could be attributed to emotion. Something special was happening tonight, and he wasn't yet sure what—nor how it would end up affecting him.

After a few moments of thought, Leiv cleared his throat, then rubbed the outside of his neck—physically pulling himself fully into the present while decisively and consciously making a point to place and fix everyone in his mind's eye.

Mentally marking the moment in time.

Then he stood up abruptly and walked across the room to the draped floor-to-ceiling window to the left of LC's massive fireplace. A fireplace where the mantle front was the secret home to his favorite of the Mojave-Stones. *Hidden in plain sight.* Knowledge shared only by him and his deceased grandparents. When in this room, the unpolished rock-looking stone would often catch Leiv's eye and fancy, causing him to make sure his facial expressions gave nothing away. This moment, he wanted to take a few more steps to stand in front of the fireplace and touch the stone. He didn't.

He did touch the heavy brocade drapes his father Everett had commissioned to keep the room dark—the sun having destroyed LC and Viola's original window hangings from the outside—and as he pulled them back, the very act enabled Leiv to follow his mind and heart where they wanted to go. It was the oddest sensation Leiv had ever had. The room, the people behind him faded from his consideration. And most welcome as he pulled the heavy floor-to-ceiling drape back, was revealed an almost black night, clear from refracted light, and star-studded.

Resolution and clarity for him, though not easy, began to come. Leiv even thought he felt the eyes of his guests boring-in on his back; it was of little consequence. Three years now, and he could finally see the journey he was on.

Illinois *to* Shiné. Logic, legality in all its cultural and political trappings—*versus*—real life consequences, innate morality, and justice in real time.

My journey. Not LC's, not Everett's. Mine. He thought he might have said the words aloud, but hoped he hadn't. Yet Leiv wasn't so completely disconnected he didn't hear Pete behind ask, "What is this cordial called?"

"It's sherry," Pastor Lloyd Apply answered fondly. "Harvey's Bristol Crème." Their voices faded back into the background.

Leiv's past life had always been about doing what was right. From his grandfather, through his dad, and through his career. But now he was indeed ready to say, *screw the rules.* He wanted to turn around and sneak a look at both Doc Walker and Glover—in addition, and though he couldn't, he also wanted to smile fondly at the absent Elizabeth-May and Mary. Indeed, he wished for the ladies presence here, tonight. He doubted, however, they would have come even if he'd asked.

Secrets, one and all.

He had suspected about Mary that first day, appreciating together her amber Hobnail Penny perfume bottle. Though Doctor Will Walker's logically causative or correlated involvement complicated the verdict. *Post Hoc, Ergo Propter Hoc—* Leiv caught himself. *What's wrong with me?* Latin logic and legal terms. *No, that's all behind me.*

And Elizabeth-May he knew about the moment he looked into Tempe's eyes. For sure, that dog had stuck the stick in the root cellar clasp. Locked Alex in for good after Elizabeth-May had conked him on the head. His canine instincts telling him the evil man constituted danger to his mistress.

For the first time in his life Leiv was abetting a murderer getting away. *Two murderers in fact.* But surprisingly, he wanted it that way—and was quite comfortable with his lawless decision. *The man of law has happily gone to the dark-side.*

Finally, he shot a quick glance Glover's way, hoping he wasn't reading his mind, but the Chief looked away abruptly. An act not in character for Glover, and Leiv wasn't sure what that was about. But he certainly wasn't going to tell Glover—*brother or not*—anything he knew about Mary or Elizabeth-May.

He dared not look at Charlie—he was some spooky kind of mind reader for sure. Worse than Glover.

Still facing a dark and clear Shiné night beyond LC's withdrawing-room window, Leiv closed his eyes, clearly seeing again Glover and himself standing on the pavement in front of Le Bric-à-Brac, Max's dead body lying on Main Street's cement sidewalk—Felliniesquely covered with Margaret's red and green tarp. He knew even then, *before* experiencing the second hobnail bottle, Mary was at the least, partly guilty. At the time, he refused to accept what he knew to be truth.

And Elizabeth May, how could he turn in his own dear cousin? Sure, she'd pushed Alex in the root cellar. Of course Tempe actually put the stick in the lock. *Post Hoc, Ergo Propter Hoc* again. Did she know about the stick? Could she have saved him? His guess, Elizabeth-May knew.

Two women. Two women he really liked. Two probable murderers—with a dog and a doctor as accomplices.

When he brought his attention back to the room, Leiv took a deep breath, turned around and faced tonight's gathering—Marilyn, Pete, and Doc Walker were the closest and right in front of him, next Margaret Deers rather regally ensconced on the love seat, then Pastor Apply in his regular chair facing the fireplace and marking the top of their circle. To Apply's right was the Edwardian nested side table he and the pastor shared many a cordial across. Of course there was his empty armchair next, then Glover strategically squeezed in between his chair and the loveseat Charlie had been sharing with David.

Leiv wanted to make a toast—but he hadn't brought his glass of sherry with him. Toasts were not something he often did—but tonight was special—and this moment in time he wanted to better appreciate, celebrate with a raised glass. *Life being lived.*

Before he could make a glassless toast—and with the words still formulating in his brain—LC's withdrawing-room's main door opened, and a grinning David Milhouse, HM, and Dobie came in. David was actually holding HM's hand as if they were teenagers, and his housekeeper was smiling in a goofy way Leiv had never seen before.

Now speechless and toast forgotten, Leiv continued to watch as Dobie sauntered over to the fireplace and laid down in her previously preferred spot on the handmade Anatolia Terrain hearth-rug. Then she closed her eyes almost immediately. *Whatever is going on isn't about to keep Dobie from her nap.*

"Decided we'd rejoin the party," David mumbled. "And it wasn't tea, but a Romani spiced cider." With a proud gesture, he held high the tumbler he was carrying in his other hand.

To Leiv's eye, "Romani Cider" looked muddy and quite unappealing. He also noticed HM was also carrying a glass in her free hand—but it looked to be filled with a honey colored liquid. He guessed, she'd chosen B&B over cider.

Leiv kept his composure, passed on his contemplated melodramatic toast, and headed back to his comfy leather armchair next to Apply. Immediately after Leiv passed behind her loveseat, Margaret crossed over and took David's previous spot next to Charlie, while graciously indicating David and Hester should share her now-vacated loveseat.

He didn't know what to think or say on the David and Hester "thing," and by the time Leiv resettled into his chair Pete asked, "What's with this story about a Mojave-Stone I heard at The Greasy Spoon?"

Leiv inclined his head innocently and didn't immediately answer. Caught off guard, he needed a couple seconds to recover—and make sure he didn't reflexively act in a way he'd later regret. Indeed, *he wanted* to look up at the hearthstones above the firebox, recognize his father's genius, *he wanted* to look over at HM and see what kind of expression she had—Guilt? Anticipation? Curiosity? *He wanted* to scan all the faces in LC's wonderful room to see if there was any interest besides Pete's. And most peculiarly, Leiv *wanted* to laugh.

167

Harvey's Bristol Cream affecting me? Most probably. But also, at that moment, he felt genuine relief flood through his body, knowing because of him, Elizabeth May and Mary Jones were in no danger of prosecution. Being an Illinois judge was long behind him. *No,* he would be declining the offer to go back to Illinois. He was just fine not being a judge. Being Leigh Cooper Rhodes's son in Shiné was quite enough.

"Does the Mojave-Stone actually exist?" Pete pressed.

Before he answered Pete, Leiv connected across the years to LC and spoke for them both. "Of course not." He spoke without hesitation, and with nary a second thought.

Then—without warning—came the sound of helicopters. Loud, insistent, and close.

Leiv stood up again and quickly headed toward the withdrawing-room doors. No words were spoken, no instructions given, yet everyone got up, and with Leiv leading the way—almost in unison as if overtaken by some other-worldly controlling device—followed him out of the withdrawing-room and down the hall to the front stained-glass double doors, with Glover as their rear-guard.

As he and they stepped out, one by one, their gazes went skyward toward a dark and mysterious Shiné starlit sky. As their little group stared into the sky above, mesmerized, it almost felt like to Leiv, a "caravan" of military helicopters, barely visible except for eerie-looking low intensity green, red, and white lights that seemed to flare slightly in the night sky. They were flying low in a procession of sorts, moving as eerie gray-looking phantoms across the pitch-black air-space above Rhodes Castle. *Heading to Twenty-nine Palms,* Leiv guessed. He wondered if Pete Lily would try to take pictures, but doubted what they were experiencing could be captured on film.

Indeed, for a few moments in time, assembled outside in their little group of sorts, in front of LC's massive front door, with no words exchanged, ignoring the realities of physical possibilities, and with *no* exceptions—all raised their arms and waved at the passing helicopter transports like little kids.

Epilogue

Pete "PL" Lily did take his "official" helicopter flyover shoot of Shiné's little piece of the Mojave—first backtracking to nearby historical and iconic Amboy, then all the way north to I-15—including Lookout Loop and Shiné Ridge. During that adventure, when Jack flew over what PL took as the trailhead for a section of the Kelso Dunes, a couple, hikers by the look of their attire, looked skyward as they flew over and waved.

He was filming of course, and consequently caught the couple as they stood at the dunes entrance in his lens-view long enough to see the woman, after her wave, next grab at and snare a solitary and largish piece of paper that seemed to be skipping along through scrub brush—heading it appeared for the pristine dunes further up the trail.

The couple appeared to take a few seconds to look at the sheet of paper, and though his helicopter moved on, Pete was almost entranced by what he was seeing and filming—and most importantly as pilot Jack continued their journey—Pete thought he saw her fold the paper and slip it into the back of her hiking companion's backpack.

Pete was surprised how much he could see from his distance above them—or thought he could see. *Well*, he could go back if he wanted and make sure; it was recorded now. *Wonder what that piece of paper was?* With further thought, Pete figured the couple was planning on depositing the paper in the closest trash. *Keeping the desert trash-free?* It was too late to see behind him, but he thought he'd noticed a trash receptacle right there next to the couple at the trailhead. So why store in her hiking companion's backpack? *Curious.*

Even more curious—Jack, unasked, headed for a moment out over the dunes, then turned around and came back over the couple, bringing them into view from a second side before continuing on course. It was like Jack had a plan of his own? *How could he?* Well, he would take a look at the film when they got back. His "photographic eye" as Charlie called it, would be able to see whatever he was *feeling* about the scene.

And as they moved on farther through the skies above the Mojave desert, Pete forgot about Jack and the couple—and just smiled from pure pleasure. For once again, he was amazed how this morning's sunrise, just like Saturday's, was bright without being blinding, colored without being saturated or intense, and sparkling without being visually confusing. *And the way it's catching the cragginess of Shiné Ridge...*just like their first morning hiking up to Douglas Chan's log cabin.

Gorgeous.

As before, it was the sound that first caught Leiv's attention. He was in Rhodes Castle's library again—at his grandfather LC's desk, ensconced in his father Everett's armchair, and lankily stretched out with his legs crossed at the ankles under the desk, his head dropped back against the chair's back, and his eyes closed.

He was contemplating events of the last couple days—in particular, the thoughts and new emotions those events had left in their metaphorical wake. Nonetheless, physical comfort and indulging in philosophical thought aside, he couldn't not get up and take a look when he heard the sound that now *seemed* like an old friend.

As expected, once at his library window, he could see the helicopter and its shadow moving across Shiné Ridge. Triggered by that image, Leiv remembered his parting and last conversation with Charlie White as the filming team finally said their goodnights—their words, the setting, the mood, all still surprisingly fresh in his mind:

"*It's funny how a movie of a book is often not the*

same," *Leiv mused to the producer.*

They were still sitting in their chairs in LC's withdrawing-room—having a final toast of sorts. A goodbye toast. The two of them.

In response to Leiv's question, Charlie turned in his chair a bit, more directly toward him, and with what looked like genuine curiosity in his eyes, asked, "Which do you usually like better?"

Leiv thought back for a moment before admitting, "Can't say. Have gone both ways."

"Do you know what distinguishes a good director from an ok one?"

"Not a clue."

Charlie White, award winning producer, director, and more, said with conviction edged in authority, "It's first arranging a story's visual aspects dramatically. Then comes filling in the story."

This morning, Leiv remembered they had then taken a couple minutes of silence Sunday night. Had he poured another aperitif? That part Leiv wasn't sure of. He did remember though, he was the one who broke the silence.

"Is that mechanics or art?"

"Art for sure." Then after a bit more quietness between them, Charlie added, "But you do need to stay true to the book." Next he'd laughed. "While in real life, you can pick and chose events to pay attention to—lie if necessary—keep secrets if necessary—change course in your life pursuits." His voice faded as if remembering something in particular.

"I would have said it's the other way around."

Charlie made an enigmatic little sound. "Real life, or a movie? Hard to tell sometimes. Aren't we all movie-makers of a sort. In our own way?"

And now, as he watched the helicopter disappear for a

long otherworldly-like moment—with its bone-and-house-rattling noise slowly fading and leaving a receding hum in its wake that somehow echoed Charlie's remembered words—Leiv wondered the same about recent events.

ACKNOWLEDGEMENTS

As always, my gratitude goes to my excellent editors—Mike Foley and Kitty Kladstrup. This story would not be published without them.

To my relatives, friends, fellow authors, and readers—thanks for your continuing words of encouragement. I can never properly say how much your support means to me.

I'm also most grateful to my Route 66 and Public Safety Writers Association (PSWA) friends and business owners who always so graciously provide information on animals, politics, law-enforcement, Route 66, and local lore. Special thanks goes to Hap Meredith, for letting Glover and his father "steal" his tattoo. And to Robert "Bob" Haig, author of *Fire Horses*, a retired Detroit Firefighter for sharing his experience and letting me borrow and modify his fire ghost-child.

And to my dear editor for so long, Virginia Moody, whose angel spirit now continues to sustain me—thank you for being my friend.

Madeline (M.M.) Gornell's mystery novels include—PSWA award winners *Uncle Si's Secret* and *Lies of Convenience* (also a Hollywood Book Festival Honorable Mention), *Death of a Perfect Man*, and *Reticence of Ravens* (a finalist for the Eric Hoffer 2011 fiction Prize, the da Vinci Eye for cover art, and the Montaigne Medal for most thought provoking book). *Counsel of Ravens* (a London Book Festival Honorary Mention and LA Book Festival Runner-Up) is her first sequel, and was a continuation of Hubert Champion's Mojave saga. Rhodes—The Movie-Maker is her second sequel, and the continuation of Leiv Rhodes's saga begun in Rhodes—The Mojave-Stone.

She continues to be inspired by historic Route 66, and this her second Rhodes novel, reflects that continuing fascination. Madeline lives with her husband and assorted canines in the Mojave High Desert near the internationally revered Route 66.

On page one hundred and two, where Leigh Cooper Rhodes explains the origin of his town's name—Shiné:

Viola likes to show our boys the stones in morning light. Sitting as they do up top of the house, mornings usually, letting the sun make them glitter, sparkle, shine. André calls it shiny, and it comes out his little mouth as shy-knee. Viola's got a soft spot for that one, and has started saying the name of our place shy-knee like the boy. She may have made shy-knee a reality, but it's little André who really named the place.

Thinking I'm gonna be changing the spelling too, and with one of them little marks at the end. Make it fancy, befitting a Leigh Cooper Rhodes kind of town.

Then he'd printed, in block letter across a whole page:

SHINÉ

www.ingramcontent.com/pod-product-compliance
Lightning Source LLC
Chambersburg PA
CBHW020908180626
46816CB00007BA/2304